Advance praise for Angie Vicars's
Treat

"A realistic story of coming out, finding love, and dealing with all the trials, pain, and passion that those things bring. I identified so totally with Gerd that at times I felt I was reading about my own past. I imagine that many women who read this will feel the same."

–Juliet Carrera, author of *Inside Out*

"*Treat* is a treat indeed–a lesbian romance with heart, a brain, and a great sense of humor. The dialogue in Vicars's debut novel sparkles with wit and sexual chemistry. *Treat*'s two immensely likeable college-age heroines, Gerd and Max, will be readily embraced by lesbian readers."

–Julia Watts, author of the novels *Wildwood Flowers*, *Phases of the Moon*, *Piece of My Heart*, *Wedding Bell Blues*, and *Mixed Blessings*

"*Treat* lives up to its name. The electricity between the two girls fairly sizzles. All the memories of girlish loving in the past–all the delicious shivers of anticipation–all the uncertainties of first love between college girls–all the pain of family estrangement because of homophobia: *Treat* treats its readers to the ever-delightful awakening of love."

–Loralee MacPike, PhD, Professor Emerita of English, California State University, San Bernardino

Treat

Alice Street Editions
Judith P. Stelboum
Editor-in-Chief

Past Perfect, by Judith P. Stelboum

Inside Out, by Juliet Carrera

Façades, by Alex Marcoux

Weeding at Dawn: A Lesbian Country Life, by Hawk Madrone

His Hands, His Tools, His Sex, His Dress: Lesbian Writers on Their Fathers, edited by Catherine Reid and Holly K. Iglesias

Yin Fire, by Alexandra Grilikhes

Treat, by Angie Vicars

Forthcoming

From Flitch to Ash: A Musing on Trees and Carving, by Diane Derrick

To the Edge, by Cameron Abbott

Egret, by Helen Collins

Extraordinary Couples, Ordinary Lives, by Lynn Haley-Banez and Joanne Garrett

Foreword

Alice Street Editions provides a voice for established as well as up-and-coming lesbian writers, reflecting the diversity of lesbian interests, ethnicities, ages, and class. This cutting-edge series of novels, memoirs, and non-fiction writing welcomes the opportunity to present controversial views, explore multicultural ideas, encourage debate, and inspire creativity from a variety of lesbian perspectives. Through enlightening, illuminating, and provocative writing, Alice Street Editions can make a significant contribution to the visibility and accessibility of lesbian writing, and bring lesbian-focused writing to a wider audience. Recognizing our own desires and ideas in print is life sustaining, acknowledging the reality of who we are, our place in the world, individually and collectively.

Judith P. Stelboum
Editor-in-Chief
Alice Street Editions

Treat Yourself!

Angie Vicars

To Jean,
I hope you enjoy Reading
this as much as I
enjoyed writing it.

Alice Street Editions

Harrington Park Press

New York · London · Oxford

This is a work of fiction. No reference to actual persons, places, or incidents is implied or should be inferred.

Published by

Alice Street Editions, Harrington Park Press®, an imprint of The Haworth Press, Inc., 10 Alice Street, Binghamton, NY 13904-1580 USA (www.HaworthPress.com).

Cover design by Thomas J. Mayshock Jr.

Library of Congress Cataloging-in-Publication Data

Vicars, Angie.
    Treat / Angie Vicars.
      p. cm.
    ISBN 1-56023-214-5 (hard)–ISBN 1-56023-215-3 (pbk.)
    I. Title.
PS3572.I24 T74 2001
813'.6–dc21

                                                00-054226

Acknowledgments

I am very glad to acknowledge assistance from the following people in making this novel a reality.

My Mom, Dad, and Brother have always encouraged my efforts as a writer and storyteller.

Amy kicked me in the butt when I wasn't writing. This novel is the result. (As you predicted, Amy, in five years I am on the phone with my editor. Well, okay, six years.)

Julia Watts gave me countless suggestions for getting published and did edits for coffee, dinner, and beer.

Judith Stelboum (one of Julia's suggestions) read this, recommended it to the publisher, and gave me ideas for the last rewrite.

Brian went sledding with me. Even though I cut the sledding scene in this, it was great research. Until I lost the feeling in my thumbs.

Paul told me, "Hey, I'm a straight white man over forty and I didn't want to put it down. It'll sell."

I worked in many bookstores over the years with friends who reassured me that one day they'd be selling my book. They were right.

The Writers' Roundtable I founded preserved my sanity and kept me accountable for finishing my work.

The Monday Night Prayer Group supported me week after week after week . . .

Several people read versions of this and gave me feedback that's much appreciated:

Keytha (twice)
Lea (twice)
Deanna
Jenny
Julie (notes on the phone)
Mary
Paul (put reinforcement tabs on several pages)
Julia (notes over coffee)
Annalee (notes at dinner)
Sara
Cali

To love another is something
like prayer and can't be planned,
you just fall into its arms because
your belief undoes your disbelief.

–Anne Sexton
''Admonitions to a Special Person''

Chapter One

The first time Max and Gerd met was in February. Knoxville was recovering from a huge storm that started as freezing rain and quickly changed to snow, dumping over a foot in a day's time. Two nights later, their car skidded in the parking lot entrance as Gerd and her fiancé, Richard, went to see Noel Coward's *Present Laughter.*

This was only the second play Gerd had seen on campus, and as they settled in their seats, Richard started explaining the set to her. Gerd smiled at him, but she wished he would stop. He had a habit of instructing her that she found terribly overbearing, although she'd never told him so. She knew the apartment backdrop was done in art deco style without his telling her.

She reminded herself of the reasons she'd said yes to his proposal at Christmas. He was very considerate, always opening doors for her and pulling out chairs. He wanted to build a two-story house with a big yard for her and their two kids. He was smart, about to graduate at the top of his class from law school. He knew what he wanted to do; he was planning to go into corporate law and was clerking over the summers in one of the downtown firms. He was handsome, too, with thick, short brown hair, very kind brown eyes, and great muscles from biking.

But there was something missing from her list: love. She wanted to love him but for some reason she couldn't explain, the best she could do so far was to like him a lot. She knew he loved her, and she intended to fall in love with him at some point, hopefully before the wedding. It would happen, she thought. He was everything she'd ever been taught to expect in a husband. Coming back to the moment, however, Gerd decided she'd had enough art deco instruction. "Didn't you say you know one of the actresses?"

"Yes, I do." A smile warmed his face. "Her name's Max Ivers, short for Maxine. She lived across the hall from me one summer. The guy who had lived there went overseas and subletted it to her. She's been getting great reviews in this."

"Her name's familiar. Maybe she was in the other play I saw. There was an actress I liked in that."

"You'd remember Max if you saw her," Richard said in a tone that sounded like bragging.

"You sound awfully sure about that," Gerd teased him.

"She's very nice looking, honey, that's all I mean. Anyway, I'll point her out to you when she comes on." He kissed her hand. "She's not as nice looking as you, of course." He kept her hand folded in his as the lights went dim. Gerd shifted, hoping her arm wouldn't go numb from the armrest jutting into it.

As a dark-haired woman made her first appearance onstage, Richard clenched Gerd's hand. That must be Max, she thought.

Just then, he leaned over. "That's Max."

Gerd studied her intently. She was tall and angular with a very graceful way of moving. As she started her lines, it was easy to be taken in by her voice. It was deep and rich. The upper-class British accent she was using sounded very smooth. Max made a double entendre and laughed as a servant poured her a drink. There was something about her, something that got Gerd's attention and made her want to keep watching. Richard was right. She would've remembered Max.

Feeling a bit hot and bothered, Gerd shifted in her seat. Sometimes she reacted like this to women, as if she had a crush on them. She had never told anyone about it. Besides, she didn't really *want* women, she always decided. She wasn't a lesbian. She just . . . what? Appreciated a beautiful woman. Yes, that was it. Appreciated them, not desired them.

So why do I keep focusing on Max more than the play? she wondered. Oh, get over it, she thought, shifting in her seat. Again.

*   *   *

Gerd was worried as she and Richard stood waiting in the theatre's green room. Richard had surprised her, asking if she wanted to meet Max in person. She hadn't even known you could do that, just go down and meet the actors.

But even though she was dying to meet Max, Gerd was also very scared. What if Max had the same effect on her in person as she did when there was an audience between them? What if Max noticed? What if Richard noticed? What if it was going to drive her crazy? Gerd decided to concentrate on looking around instead.

Richard started telling her that the green room was where the actors waited to go on and where they lounged around between classes. Lounged was a good word, Gerd thought. The room was filthy. The dark green carpet had gum ground into it. The hard-candy green walls had dried coffee splashes on them. The chairs and the bulletin boards were ratty. The sink and cabinets in the corner hadn't been cleaned in ages. How did anyone stand it in here?

Just as Max came walking through the doorway, Gerd froze. She felt weak. Uh-oh, maybe this was desire she was feeling after all.

Max was even more striking out of costume and up close. She had long, thick, curly black hair and smooth skin with an honest-to-God rosy glow. She was wearing a big white T-shirt, along with jeans that were worn through in many places. And she was barefoot. Her appearance was absolutely the opposite of everything Gerd had been taught about how to dress, but she thought Max looked fabulous.

Max quickly smiled as Richard came toward her, catching her up in a tight hug. "You sneak. You should've told me you were coming," she said, kissing him on the cheek. "It's so good to see you."

Gerd was wondering just how well Richard and Max really knew each other. He'd said they were friends, but Gerd sensed an intimacy between them that seemed stronger than friendship. She was also wondering if Max's feet were cold. Wasn't she afraid she'd get sick going barefoot when it was so cold outside? And where were the rest of her clothes? Surely she had more than a T-shirt.

Max stepped back, looked right at her and smiled. All the hairs on Gerd's body simultaneously rose. Desire, Gerd knew it. That's what she felt. She wanted to run, but she knew she couldn't have made her feet move. It was like being struck by an electric current, she imagined. A tingling numbness settled over her.

Then she heard Richard talking again. "Max, I'd like you to meet my fiancée. This is Gertrude Mackenzie. She goes by Gerd. She's always thought that sounds better than Gert."

Max held out her hand. "I think it sounds better too. It's nice to meet you. Gerd."

"You too," Gerd managed to say, glancing at her own hand hanging by her side. She willed it to move. Miraculously, it did. She didn't manage a handshake, really. She just lifted her hand. Max's hand was incredibly warm and smooth. Desire made Gerd's knees feel weak.

Max and Richard started talking, saying something about the show and someone they both knew and how the semester was going. Gerd just stood there, feeling dumbfounded.

Then a man's voice was calling to Max from the dressing room. "Max-a-million, my angel, your hair needs cutting. Chop chop."

"I'll be right there," Max called back, then grinned at the surprised looks on Richard's and Gerd's faces. "Taylor's trimming my hair before we go eat."

This woman is so utterly different from me, Gerd thought. She's absolutely fascinating.

"Listen, we have to get going anyway," Richard said. "I'll give you a call soon. I'm having a little party after midterms, kind of a stress reliever. You're invited."

"I'll keep it in mind," Max assured him. They started out of the room, with Max just standing there watching them. But Gerd could've sworn Max was watching her more. Or maybe Gerd just wanted her to. What's with me? she wondered, as she concentrated on putting one foot in front of the other. "Hey, wait a minute," Max called. "You're Richard's fiancée, right?"

Richard turned back with a big grin on his face, starting to talk before Gerd even opened her mouth. "She sure is. After I pass the bar, I'm taking her down the aisle."

"Well," Max began, and looked Gerd right in the eyes as if to emphasize that she was talking to her, "I didn't see your ring. Has Mr. Won't-Let-You-Get-a-Word-in-Edgewise given you one yet?"

"Oh. Yes, he has." Gerd walked over to show her. Max lifted Gerd's hand until she could see the ring very closely. She must be 5'8" or 5'9", Gerd thought as she looked up.

"This is very pretty," Max told her. "I haven't seen one with emeralds around the diamond before."

"They're my favorite stones, emeralds."

Max looked over the ring, down into Gerd's eyes again. Gerd's breath caught. "Are they birthstones?"

Exhale, Gerd thought. Exhale. "I don't know. I mean, I don't think so. I mean, they could be but they're not mine. Not my birthstones anyway."

Max grinned at her. "When is your birthday, Gerd?"

Why did she want to know that? Gerd wondered, though it thrilled her anyway. "January fourth."

"You're a Capricorn," Max said, finally letting go of Gerd's hand. An odd, tingling sensation ran up Gerd's arm. She wanted Max to hold her hand again. Richard took it instead. "That means you think with your head first and you prefer fitting in more than standing out."

"That's me, all right. What sign are you, Max?"

"I'm a Pisces. I think with this first." She pointed to her heart. "Capricorns help me balance."

Richard glanced at his watch. "Max, it was great to see you again," he said with a sigh that suggested it was late.

"You too, Richard. And it was very nice to meet you, Gerd."

"You too," Gerd told her, taking one last look at her before she and Richard went out the door. Desire, that was what she felt. She knew it. Uh-oh.

This is crazy, rehearsing this show while we're still doing *Present Laughter*, Max was thinking. I shouldn't have promised Roger I'd do this. I'd really like to be at home tonight, just one night. I'm never home until late at night. Who knows? Maybe Gerd would call. I have no idea why she would call, but who knows?

Something hit her in the head and bounced on the floor. Feeling dazed, Max finally realized that it was a script. She looked in the direction of her attacker.

Raney was shaking her head. "It's your line, Hepburn."

"What line?"

The rest of the cast was looking either pissed or tired. "We may as well be rehearsing with a blow-up doll, Rog," Raney said to the student director.

"Decorum, ladies, please," Roger vamped in an upper-class English accent before Max could fire back. "Let's take a break."

"How long?" Raney asked.

"That depends on what takes longer–Max regaining her concentration or me slitting my wrists and bleeding to death in our teeny tiny restroom."

"I'll get it back," Max assured him, rolling her eyes.

"Do we need to talk?" Roger asked in a genuinely concerned tone, as she passed him.

"No. I'm just distracted by my life right now. I'll re-group." Roger nodded understandingly. Max went outside, but before she even got across the street, she heard familiar footsteps following her.

"Hey, alter ego, wait up." Raney caught up to her. They called each other "alter ego" sometimes because it was the name they used when they played at clubs. Saturday night, 9:00, Alter Egos at Tomato Head for a three-dollar cover. Their music was partly original and partly cover songs, a mix of folk, blues, and country on acoustic guitars, inspired by the Indigo Girls, although they did their best not to imitate them. "Who's gotten under your skin?"

As a gust of wind blew, the dogwood trees at the top of the hill swayed until they half bent over. Across the street at Hess Hall, a towel blew out of a window and went spiraling through the air until it was forced against the bricks. "How'd you know someone's gotten under my skin?" Max asked.

Raney turned her head so her wavy blond hair would blow behind her shoulders. "Oh, I guess it's that dreamy, distracted . . ."

"Don't say it."

". . . giddy . . . ow . . . look on your face while you're missing your lines."

"Look, it really doesn't matter who she is. Okay?"

"Why? Is she straight?"

Max stared down at her feet as the sidewalk turned downhill and grew broken in places. "Well, she's engaged to Richard so she might as well be, no matter how I feel."

"No shit." Raney was one of the few people who knew that Max had slept with Richard once a couple years ago. "Did you get any vibes from her?"

"Yes, I did. Some very strong ones, I think."

"Good God, Max, from Richard's fiancée? You're sure?"

"I'm sure *I* felt something. I *think* she did. I don't know."

"Good God, Max."

"Yes, that's right, Raney, God and Jesus and the Holy Mother and *everything* else. What do I do?"

"What do you want to do?"

"I want to do her, that's the problem."

"So what's stopping you, besides Richard?"

"Screw Richard," Max said, laughing at her own joke. "Oh wait. I tried that already. It just didn't do it for me."

"You're so bad, Max."

"Actually, Richard wasn't bad at all. I've always liked him. He's just not my type. Well, not my gender. Anyway, let's see. What's

stopping me? I guess the problem is that I'm not into dragging
people out of the closet. I'd rather they come."

"Max, quit making innuendoes. You can say this is bothering
you."

"This is bothering me."

"That's better. So besides the engagement, and the fact that
she's probably straight, is anything else stopping you?"

"Isn't that enough for you, woman?"

"It's more than enough for me. But I know you."

Max sighed, meaning to be dramatic, but it came out sounding
rather pitiful. "She's out of my league, Rain. That's the plain truth
of it. She looks like a Laura Ashley model and you can just tell her
family tree goes back to the Mayflower. I'll bet she drives a Beamer.
I'll bet she's the double-legacied secretary in the richest sorority on
campus."

"Why'd she catch your eye then?"

"She's gorgeous, for one thing. She's got golden blond hair that
curls all over, cut in a bob. The most electric blue eyes I've ever
seen. They're even more blue than yours."

"They can't be more blue than mine," Raney said. She stopped
walking. "Look again."

Max barely had to tilt her head to make the comparison.
"Sorry, Rain, they're more blue. And it's not from contacts,
either."

"Damn."

"Anyway, she has this hourglass figure, you know, actual curves
that fill out her clothes. Little hands and feet. A great smile that
makes her eyes crinkle. She smells like CK One, which I suddenly
like a lot more than I ever did before. And . . ." Max actually
stopped walking.

"And what?" Raney demanded.

"And zing. Oh my God, you just would not believe the zing.
From the minute I saw her with Richard I couldn't take my eyes
off her. It's like there's electricity coming out of her pores or

something. I mean, I was afraid to touch her hand and then I was afraid to let it go."

"So, why did you?" Raney asked, tugging Max's hand so she'd start walking again.

"Why'd I what?" Max pulled her hand away.

"Touch it or let it go?"

"I was looking at her engagement ring."

"You didn't palm it, did you?" Max smacked Raney's arm. "Was it stunning?"

"Of course it was, a diamond with emeralds around it. I can't compete with that."

As they reached the Golden Roast Coffee House, Raney opened the door. The smells of freshly brewed coffee and espresso came wafting through the air, causing Max to inhale deeply when they stopped at the dessert counter. A Turtle cheesecake, an Amaretto cheesecake, and an Irish Cream cheesecake were on the top row, with a lemon layer cake, a red velvet cake, a Black Forest cake, and a mocha torte underneath. "I've got to have some of that mocha torte," Max announced.

"Not me, I want the lemon layer cake," Raney said. They walked around the counter to get in line. "So why am I just now hearing about Gerd?"

"Because I've been trying to stop thinking about her. I mean, I can't get what I want out of this situation. I'm just torturing myself."

As they moved up to next in line, Raney looked right at Max. "You can't stop thinking about her though, can you?"

"No. Shit, Rain." Max looked away, running her hand through her hair with a hopeless expression. "What should I do?"

Raney was quiet for a moment, looking thoughtful, then she said, "Are you absolutely certain there's no chance she could be interested in you? I mean, do you know this for a fact?"

Trying to hide her surprise, Max said, "Well, no. I guess not."

"Then give it a shot, Max. You and Richard aren't close

anymore and I can't see what else you've got to lose besides his . . . I guess it's still friendship."

"My mind," Max suggested, laughing a little crazily, trying to break the tension. "I could lose my mind."

"Don't let something that small hold you back," Raney advised her with a wicked smile.

Chapter Two

Gerd felt as if she were going to suffocate. Richard's after-midterms party had begun to seem like a total façade to her. She was pretending to be friends with almost all of these people. But who were they anyway? Richard's friends, many she knew and only a few she liked. Two of her good girlfriends were here, but ninety-five percent were people she'd rather not spend an evening with.

And to make matters more complicated, something totally unexpected had happened. Max had come. This wasn't Max's crowd and Gerd had been sure that she wouldn't show, that she was just being polite to Richard in the green room that night. Well, so much for that assumption. Gerd had caught herself staring at Max a few times. The last time, Max, trapped in a conversation with a guy Gerd thought of as Statistical Steve, had caught her. A blush had gone across Gerd's face all the way into her hair.

In the bathroom, Gerd turned to the mirror so she'd know when her blush had dulled. Did she look too preppy? she wondered, thinking that wasn't Max's style at all. She was wearing a light blue J. Crew pullover shirt with a darker blue cardigan sweater, a matching long skirt and Liz Claiborne flats. As she straightened her sweater, she thought, no, not too preppy. Then she looked at the gold buckles she'd stuck on the flats. Who was she kidding? Too preppy. Maybe she could stay in here the rest of the night. Someone jiggled the door. "Just a minute," she called.

"Who is that?" Statistical Steve called back. Why did he want to know? Oh well, at least Max had gotten away from him. Gerd wondered where to go now as she unlocked the door.

Richard's bedroom, that should be a good place to hide for awhile. He'd shut the door because he'd put everyone's coats on the bed. She didn't know why it mattered if people saw their coats not being worn, but she'd ceased to question Richard's "Richard-isms" aloud. (The night she'd asked why he insisted that she put the dishes in the drainer in a certain way, she'd almost nodded off during his long-winded explanation.) In fact, now she was grateful the bedroom door was shut. Once she was inside she closed her eyes, sighing with relief.

Feeling much more relaxed, she opened her eyes to . . . oh no. Her heart started to pound. There was Max, looking so comfortable barefoot, in a baggy sweater and jeans. She was leaning on the windowsill, but looking back at Gerd. She's been looking at the view of the city, Gerd told herself. Her being here has nothing to do with me. From fifteen flights up you could see a terrific view of Knoxville, which was one of Gerd's favorite things about Richard's apartment. In fact, he kidded her that she only really loved him for his view. Could that be the truth? She never got this excited when she caught him at the windowsill.

Don't dwell on that, she thought. After dark, Gerd liked to imagine the city lights as diamonds on a spread of black velvet, and she wondered if Max did too. No, she wouldn't think that. It was too corny. Max was still looking at her.

With a smile, Max finally looked out the window again. "I love this view. It was the best thing about these apartments. I used to sublet across the hall and come over here to look out."

"I like it too. I'm sorry I burst in. I didn't know you were in here."

"It's okay. I don't mind sharing." Max took a deep breath, hoping that her nervousness didn't show, and moved down so Gerd could have her own window.

Gerd looked out without leaning on the sill. "I just got so hot in there and someone's in the bathroom." She laughed, wondering if she sounded as silly as she felt. "I think the wine's gone to my head."

"Wine can certainly get to you sometimes," Max said. "It usually makes me sleepy."

"It does that to me too, sometimes." Gerd paused. She wanted to say something else, something clever or witty, but she felt so distracted. I'm straight, she thought again. Why am I reacting to Max like this? Like a giddy schoolgirl with my true love under the bleachers during the game? That's how I feel, excited and tongue-tied and half-crazy.

Looking over at Gerd, Max saw an expression on her face that she could only describe as helplessness. Say something, she thought. Give her some indication that you're attracted. How many more chances will you have? "Gerd, you know what? You look like you want to get out of here. I mean, out of this party."

"Why do you say that?" Gerd asked, surprised that Max had seen through her.

"Well, maybe I noticed because I'm an actress and I'm trained to read body language."

"What's my body language saying exactly?"

"Um, just that you're uncomfortable."

"But Max, how could I be uncomfortable? This is Richard's apartment." But Gerd knew. Max could tell that she wasn't comfortable. The question was, could Max tell how nervous and excited Gerd was to find her in the room? She snuck a sideways look at her. Damn, Max was looking at her again. Maybe she was feeling the same way. Was that possible too?

Max was wondering if Gerd could tell how attracted she was. Every time Gerd looked at her, Max felt her expression slide into a smirk, sure she was caught. Did Gerd feel attracted too? Was that why she blushed? There was something going on with both of them, between them. Wasn't there? "I know it's his apartment but these are mostly his friends, right?" she finally managed to ask.

"Yes, that's true. Except for my friends Cat and Leah, we're surrounded by law students."

Max smiled. "Are they ganging up on you?"

"No, it's not that exactly. I'm just not fitting in with them, I'm afraid."

"What will you do when you're married to him? You'll be surrounded by lawyers."

Gerd laughed again, running her hands through her hair. "I don't know. I'm a little worried about that, to tell you the truth."

"Maybe you should plan a strategy."

"Oh God," Gerd sighed, letting her eyes go shut for a minute, "I don't think I can bring myself to do it." When she opened her eyes again she was looking right into Max's gorgeous green ones. Desire coursed through her, and Max had to be feeling the same way because she kept looking right at her. In fact, she was bending toward her and . . .

Max kissed her.

At first, Gerd thought it was just going to be a quick touch of the lips. But it went on. They began to move into each other, turning their heads until Gerd opened her mouth to meet Max's tongue. Gerd pressed Max even harder to her and a deep moan came from far down in her throat. When they finally broke off, Gerd felt she'd collapse if Max let go of her. They were both breathing hard. It was only when she saw the closed door that Gerd started worrying maybe someone would come in and catch them.

"I couldn't help that," Max blurted. "You're why I'm at this party, Gerd. I've wanted to do that since the night I met you. I can't get you off my mind. I think I'm going crazy. You're Richard's fiancée and he's my friend and I know you're supposed to be straight but I swear there's something going on here."

"There is," Gerd breathed. "But I'll be damned if I know what to make of it."

"Me either," Max admitted. "I think I should go now. I have an idea, though."

"What's that?"

"Why don't you come to my place later? We can talk."

"Later tonight, you mean?"

"Uh-huh."

"I can't," Gerd said weakly. "I promised to help Richard with this party. I mean, clean up and all that."

"I stay up really late. You can still come by. I mean, if you want to. Just to talk. I'm not trying to seduce you, I swear."

Gerd thought about it. Part of her wanted to go with Max right now. But a more rational part of her was still completely shocked by what she'd just done and how much she'd enjoyed it. "Max, I can't make any promises. I'm not really a late-night person and I have no idea what time we'll be done. Plus, Richard probably thinks I'm staying here." Gerd took a deep breath and thought about the feel of Max's lips. She'd said no seduction. Could Gerd trust her? Could she trust herself? She didn't think she was quite ready to become a lesbian overnight. "Where do you live?" she finally asked.

"You know in the Fort which one is the Mill House, right?" Gerd nodded. Almost everyone that went to the University of Tennessee knew that in Fort Sanders, the neighborhood by the campus, there was a house called the Mill House. It had a wooden water mill wheel on the side of it even though there was no water anywhere near it and there never had been. "I live in the back apartment, number five. I'll be at home." Max got her coat off the bed, looking around until she found her moccasins.

"Bye," Gerd said, at a loss for further words. Max looked as if she were going to walk back over to her.

"See you," she said instead, going out and pulling the door shut behind her.

Gerd pressed the back of her hand to her mouth. She'd been kissed plenty of times before and a few of the people had as much skill as Max. But this was the first time she'd ever understood the expression "melt your knees."

Chapter Three

As she turned onto the street that ran behind the Mill House, Gerd wished she were more used to driving in Fort Sanders. It was arranged in blocks and the streets were numbered, which seemed easy enough. But there were so many one-way streets that she'd driven four blocks out of her way before realizing she could've gotten to Max's in three turns.

It was two a.m. She could hardly believe she was doing this so late. Richard had been very surprised when she got her coat and her keys. She'd said she didn't feel well, but yes, she would be fine, and no, she hadn't had too much to drink. "I'm just going to go home to crash, honey," she'd told him. "I'll call you tomorrow."

When she had kissed him goodbye, she'd wondered if the taste of Max lingered on her lips. But that couldn't be. Max hadn't been wearing any lipstick or perfume.

Now here Gerd was, driving in the opposite direction from home, definitely tired and maybe a little worse for the wine after all. Maybe I'm going crazy, she thought, kissing a lesbian in the bedroom of my fiancé's apartment. And what on earth am I going to accomplish coming here to see Max? What are we going to talk about? What's going on between us? All there's been is a kiss. That doesn't mean anything. Does it? She'll want it to. Won't she? But that's not what I want. Is it? What if it is?

A back porch light shone, barely illuminating the trademark mill wheel. That must be the light at Max's apartment, Gerd thought. A black Jeep was parked in the grass. Richard had said something at the party about Max driving a Jeep. Gerd parked, took a deep breath, then another, then another, then finally got out of her car and went across the street. Her shoes were loud on the wooden porch. Yes, this was Max's apartment. There was the brass number five on the door. She pulled the screen open, making a face at the squeaky hinges as she knocked. After a moment, the door opened to Max smiling at her.

Gorgeous green eyes, oh God, Max has the most gorgeous green eyes, Gerd thought.

"Hi. I'm glad you came." Max paused, waiting for a reply.

"Sure," Gerd finally said, although it wasn't what she meant to say at all.

"Come in. I just made coffee. Do you want some?"

"I could really use it." The kitchen was so spacious that Gerd was envious. The sink and cabinets were all along one side, ending in an "L" shape with the refrigerator. The opposite side was open space with only a two-person wooden table and chairs filling it. But the colors . . . Gerd hoped they weren't Max's doing. All the cabinets were painted primary yellow and the doors were as orange as the clothes of UT fans.

"I didn't paint this," Max said as she opened a cabinet full of mugs and glasses. "Sometimes I think I'll redo it. But it's such a good conversation topic this way."

"Obviously," Gerd said, breaking into a grin. Max had changed into sweatpants and a T-shirt with an unbuttoned flannel nightshirt over it. As Gerd watched her pour coffee, she noticed again how gracefully Max moved. She seemed so at ease with herself. Gerd wished that she felt so comfortable inside her own skin.

"Let's sit in the den. It's right through there."

"Okay." Gerd went through the doorway into the next room. Her eyes took in many different things at once. There were bookshelves spilling over everywhere. Moving closer, she could see novels and history and plays, and there were far more things she couldn't see because they were stuffed so far back. There was a huge wooden, what was it, a wardrobe, a china cabinet? Gerd couldn't tell. It had wooden doors that were shut. It seemed too nosy to open them. Framed prints hung on the walls, a couple O'Keeffes along with a Monet. The prints were common ones that could be picked up at a college art sale and the frames were

inexpensive plastic, but they still implied a sense of good taste. The
coffee table was stacked with mail and magazines and handwritten
music. Multiple CD holders were spilling over with all kinds of . . .

"I'm putting the milk and sugar on the table so you can get
what you want." Max thanked God that she'd carried both things
in without breaking them. It had taken her a few minutes just to
find the spoons.

Gerd turned, feeling self-conscious again. "Thanks, this coffee
smells great." She fumbled with her purse for what felt like eons
before she set it on the floor. "Ouch," she said as she sat on the
edge of a futon with a crimson and black Southwestern pattern
that seemed much more Max's style than the kitchen.

"What's wrong?" Max was sitting across from her in a cushy
blue armchair, sipping her coffee.

"There's something under me." Gerd found that what jabbed her
was the edge of the Rickie Lee Jones CD *Flying Cowboys*. There
was also a paperback called *Patience and Sarah*.

"Sorry about that," Max apologized as Gerd put them on the
table. "I tend to lay things wherever I'm not."

"That's okay. I'd rather be poked by Rickie Lee Jones than
Ozzy Osbourne, I guess."

A smirk crossed Max's face. "That was a great one liner."

Gerd was quiet for a split second until she realized what Max
meant. "Oh, I was only funny accidentally." She immediately
wished she'd taken credit for being clever.

Max shrugged. "You still made me laugh. I'm glad you decided
to come."

Tired and nervous as she was, Gerd knew that this was the time
to end their pleasant small talk. "What did you want to talk
about?"

"Well . . ." Max paused. Am I sure? Can I do this? I've gone
too far to turn back now, haven't I? Yes. "How do you feel about
that kiss?"

"I guess I'm . . . alarmed."

"Alarmed that you did it or that you enjoyed it?"

"Both." That was an honest answer but Gerd also felt as if she should tell Max what she wanted to hear. As the oldest child, she'd always felt pressured to please everyone and do the right thing at the same time. But sometimes those two things conflicted. It felt like they were conflicting now. What am I doing here? she wondered. I can't do this. I've lost my mind. I can't be kissing some woman I barely know. I'm engaged to Richard. Gerd set her coffee on the table. "I'm sorry, Max. I think I owe you an apology."

"For what?"

"For considering . . . this. I mean, don't get me wrong, I enjoyed that kiss, but I . . ."

"You're not really attracted to women? Is that what you're telling me?" Max asked, feeling a lump rise in her throat.

Gerd looked away. "No, it's not that exactly." Damn. She looked back at Max. "I am attracted to them. I don't know why, but I am. It's just that I . . . I just can't live this way. I've never told anyone this. I can't believe I'm saying this to you."

Max set her coffee down too. Be careful, she thought. Don't get overzealous and push her when she's not ready yet. "Maybe you'll feel better if you just get it out. Besides, I don't know any of your friends except Richard and I don't think I'll be sharing this with him."

That irony made Gerd grin a little. Max grinned in return. "I do have feelings for women sometimes and I think about them, but I don't think that makes me gay."

"Why doesn't it?" Max asked gently. "I'm just asking. I'm not accusing you."

"Because I can't be gay."

"Do you mean that you can't believe that possibility or that you can't accept it?"

"I don't know what I mean. I don't know." Gerd stopped, took a breath and tried to collect her thoughts. "I have a thing for women. I've always had a thing for women. But that's not acceptable. It's not an acceptable way to live. My family would die.

They'd just die. So I can't be gay. It won't work. Do you see what I mean?"

"Gerd, have you ever slept with a woman?" Max asked, sounding as casual as possible. "I'm asking because you have so much conflict about being attracted to them. I'm wondering if there's some guilt at work here? Or are you worried because you know that your family's conservative?"

Gerd's face turned red as she stared at the floor. How could Max guess what she'd done in her younger days? How? She'd always covered it up so carefully. Well, she was giving herself away now, she thought. She forced herself to look up again. "When I was in middle school . . . this girl and I, she was a good friend of mine, we . . . fooled around . . . a few times when she stayed over. But it didn't mean anything. We never even went all the way. We didn't know how. I was young. I was just seeing what sex was all about."

Clearly, it meant much more to her than she'd ever admitted. How do I help her accept that? Max wondered. "Do you still think about her?"

"Sometimes."

"Ever dream about her?"

"Every once in awhile."

"Want someone to make you feel that good again?"

"Of course."

That blush was back full force. "Gerd," Max began, looking across and refusing to look away until Gerd met her eyes, "what if you are gay? I'm not saying I know you are. But it seems to me there's a possibility you are and your mind's not made up. Please don't take this the wrong way, but are you sure you should marry Richard?"

"No, I'm not sure. I've just been pretending." Gerd immediately felt as though a weight had lifted from her. "But I do feel attracted to Richard. What does that mean that I can be attracted to him and to women? In fact, I get the feeling that you're attracted to Richard too. Am I right?"

"I think it's natural to have attractions to people of both sexes," Max answered, after a moment of reacting privately to Gerd having noticed what she called her "Richard thing." "In fact, I hope this doesn't offend you, I slept with Richard one night and I've slept with a few other men. Those have been good experiences for me. But I prefer women. I know that."

"Do you think I really want women too?" Gerd asked. "I mean, how do I know?"

"What makes you more hot and bothered, men or women?" Max asked her in turn, thinking that Gerd didn't even come back to the "Richard thing."

"I'm not sure. What do I do that makes you think I'd prefer women?"

"Well, you fooled around with that girl growing up. You say you can't be this way but you don't say you're not. I've caught you watching me several times and I haven't seen you watching Richard." Gerd nodded for Max to continue. "The way you kissed me tonight was, um . . . let's just say I had to come home and change panties."

"Oh God, Max," Gerd blurted, blushing furiously.

"It's the truth. And then there's just this chemistry I feel between us. I was afraid it was just coming from me, but when you kissed me I started to think you must feel it too." Max was waiting for an answer but Gerd looked as if she didn't know what to say. "Do you feel something?"

Taking a deep breath, Gerd realized that as scared as she felt, she wanted to tell the truth. "Yes, I do feel something for you, Max. I'm just not sure what I feel or exactly what I'm willing to do about it. If anything. I need time to think."

"I understand. Besides, I'm not into pressuring people. Take your time, Gerd. You shouldn't rush into anything, no matter what you decide to do."

"I'd better go," Gerd said, getting to her feet. "Thank you for the coffee." Even as flustered as she was discussing this, her manners kicked in.

Max followed Gerd through the kitchen, reaching to unlock the door for her. "Gerd, I'll say one last thing. Even if I weren't attracted to you, I'd still offer my time if you need to talk. Don't hesitate to call me."

"Are you sure?" Gerd asked, looking up at Max even though she was half afraid that seeing the look in her eyes would make her want to stay. "I mean, are you sure you want a sexually confused, overdressed business major hanging out in your living room?"

Max smiled. It was such a warm expression that it lit up her whole face. "Yes, if you're sure you want to hang out with a shabbily dressed, guitar-playing, lesbian actress."

"Can I let you know?" Gerd breathed, with her pulse pounding in her ears.

"I hope you do," Max told her, kissing her lips with a touch as light as a feather. "My number's not in the book. It's 673-DOGS."

"I'll be in touch," Gerd murmured, willing her legs to get her to her car. Somehow, they did.

Chapter Four

By the next weekend, Gerd had holed up in her apartment. Her sexual identity had become such a major issue for her that she hadn't answered her phone, hadn't gotten dressed, hadn't even brushed her hair. Almost all she had done was lie on the couch with the TV on, paying no attention to what was playing, thinking instead about who she was and what gender she preferred to date.

That week, following her talk with Max, she'd tried to go on with her life as though she could contemplate change without letting it affect her. But it didn't work. Right in the middle of doing something she'd think, My tongue was in Max Ivers's mouth. It made her confused, made her blush, and made her horny. She squeezed her legs together a lot to combat the horniness, amused at the way it didn't help at all.

Then she'd remember years ago, kissing Maggie when they were at the stables and being so excited she couldn't sleep that night. Maybe this was how lesbians felt. Maybe she was a lesbian. But she just wasn't ready for that.

What she did finally decide was that she loved Richard but she wasn't in love with him. And now was a much better time to own up to it than later. She could imagine going down the aisle to him, being married to him, and even having his children. But the thoughts made her cringe because she knew deep down that wasn't what she really wanted to do. Thinking about it now, she realized she'd never be able to pull it off, acting like she fit into what her family and Richard expected from her. She'd go crazy, start screaming in the middle of some bridal shower without being able to stop.

On Friday night, hoping she could act as sure as she felt, she went to Richard's. She got her first test when he opened the door with such an excited look. It was understandable. He hadn't seen her all week. In fact, she was glad to see him too, she found. Her attraction to him wasn't simply gone. But as he started to kiss her, she turned her head to the side so that he only caught her on the cheek. Turning away from his surprised look, she dropped her coat on the couch before he could make her at home.

"You're a sight for sore eyes," he told her as she sat. "I've been reading so many case histories I think mine have crossed."

"I thought there was something funny looking about you."

"Listen, do you want to go get something to eat? Or I could make something. I've got . . ."

"Richard, um . . . I don't want anything to eat. Why don't you sit down? I need to talk to you."

"Okay." He sat by her, looking puzzled. "What's going on, Gerd? This sounds serious."

"I haven't been available this week because I've been doing a lot of thinking."

"About what?"

"About myself. And about myself with you." He looked so worried that for a moment she considered taking back what she'd said and just going to dinner with him instead. But she knew she'd already said too much. There was no going back now.

"Don't tell me you think there's something wrong with us?"

"I'm so sorry, Richard, but I think there is."

"What on earth is it, Gerd? I can't imagine but if you'll just tell me I can . . ."

"Well no, see, the thing is, you can't. You can't do anything about this because I think I might be . . . I mean I could be . . . I mean there's a possibility I'm gay." Gerd sat there for a moment, just needing to acknowledge the fact that she'd said it.

"What?" he said as though she were crazy.

"I know it's the last thing you'd expect to hear from me . . ."

"Of course it is. Gerd, you're not gay." He shook his head, grinning at her as if he thought she were just being silly. "This is about Max, isn't it? I've seen you looking at her. I'm not blind.

Honey, lots of people have crushes on Max, believe me. It doesn't mean you're a lesbian.''

What had she expected? Richard paid a lot of attention to her. Of course he'd noticed she felt something for Max. "Richard, sometimes I wish it were as simple as a crush, but it's not.''

"Excuse me?''

"No, what I mean is that Max is the one who called my attention to this. But I don't think I'm gay because I have feelings for her. I think I'm gay because I have feelings for women. She's not the first. And I may not be able to ignore my feelings anymore.''

"For God's sake, Gerd,'' he said, his voice rising for the first time, "what did Max say to you?''

"Max didn't turn me into a lesbian,'' she told him, noticing that her voice had risen too. "She asked me the same thing you did, why was I looking at her like that? And that's what made me realize that I've been working double overtime my whole life to hide the way I feel and try to make it go away. But it's not working. There I was at the party wearing the engagement ring you gave me and I was looking at her anyway.''

"Yes, but Gerd, that doesn't mean you're gay. Max is an attractive person, that's all. I may want to kill her after this, but . . .''

"You're not listening to me,'' Gerd cut in. "I don't think this is just because of Max. This has been going on my whole life. There have been plenty of parties with Max's. I just never did anything about it before.'' Oh no, she thought. Why did I have to say it that way?

"What did you do about her?'' Richard demanded. "What does that mean?''

"That's not how I meant to put it, all right?''

"C'mon, Gerd, tell me what you did about her. I think I have a right to know.''

"I didn't sleep with her, except now I doubt that you'll believe that.''

"You're right. It's beginning to sound a lot like she seduced you."

"Well, that really isn't what happened. I wish you would believe me."

"I'll tell you what I really can't believe," he said putting his hands to his head. "I can't believe this is happening to me. I introduce you to the only lesbian I know and a week later you're telling me you think you're queer too."

The word "queer" made her cringe. The angry way he said it sounded so ugly. Since she'd caught him by surprise, though, she decided to just get on with what she needed to say. "Look, Richard, I came over here tonight to tell you what's been going on. It's not that I don't have feelings for you. In fact, I love you, but I had to admit something to myself and now I have to admit it to you. I'm not in love with you. It's not because of something you didn't do or something someone else did. It's because even though I tried, that's just not how I feel toward you. So I'm giving your ring back. This wedding wouldn't be the right thing for either one of us."

"I'm so glad I could help you come to that decision, Gerd. Tell Max I said hi. Tell her I said way to fucking go."

Several angry responses went through her head but she kept them there. "I think it's time for me to leave." She stood quickly, grabbed her coat, left the ring box on the end table and went out the door. Will he try to come after me? she wondered. But as she got farther away the door stayed shut and a thought suddenly occurred to her. His bedroom, with that beautiful view, was where she and Max had first kissed. She'd never be able to go back there again. Shit. She managed to drive home, put on her bedclothes and crawl under the covers.

Now it was two days later, according to *CNN Headline News*.

Gerd knew word about their broken engagement had gotten out by the messages her friends had left on her machine. She also knew, thanks to Cat's message, that Richard had been yelling at Max outside the theatre. But she didn't know if Max had yelled back, or if they had managed to talk, or if he'd blustered off. Any of those things might have happened.

Moving down the hallway slowly, she stopped by her phone. Sighing, she wondered if she had the strength to do this. I've got to, she thought. I've put it off for too long already.

Praying that Max wasn't home, she picked up the phone and dialed 673-DOGS, which she hadn't been able to forget, even without writing it down. It rang a few times and then, thankfully, her machine picked up. "Hi, Max. It's Gerd. I heard about Richard yelling at you. I just wanted to tell you . . . well, I was going to tell you myself I gave the ring back but I couldn't figure out how and then . . . I just didn't think he'd do that. I hope it wasn't too bad. Anyway, I'm sorry you found out like that. I'll be in touch. Sometime. Bye."

Gerd leaned against the wall for a moment. What must Max be thinking about all this? That Gerd had broken off her engagement for her? That she'd come out? And wouldn't Max say that message was terribly lame? It explained nothing. Gerd looked across the room at her couch. Suddenly, she didn't want to go over there and lie down again. What do I want to do? she asked herself. What if I'm losing my mind? I have to talk to someone. She picked up the phone again.

Cat and Leah were saying something to each other when Gerd opened her front door.

"Hey you," Cat said, giving her a big hug. Both her friends were dressed in their typical turtlenecks, blazers, jeans, and loafers. Gerd, still in her bedclothes, but with her hair brushed at least, thought she must be a sorry sight.

"Are you hanging in there?" Leah asked, as she hugged Gerd too.

"I don't know what I'm doing."

"So," Cat said, "let's figure it out."

Gerd sat on the couch, picking up her twisted blanket so they could join her. There was a long pause while she tried to decide where to begin. They waited patiently. "For starters," she finally said, "I never was in love with Richard, but I was trying very hard to be."

"Well, you didn't fool either one of us," Cat told her.

"I didn't?"

Leah shook her head but didn't speak. "No," Cat paused, "we were just afraid to call you on it."

"Why were you afraid?" Gerd asked, thinking there was almost nothing Cat was afraid to discuss.

Leah looked at Cat. Cat turned back to Gerd. "Let's get to that in a minute."

"So what made you actually decide to give the ring back to him?" Leah wanted to know.

"Were you surprised?" Gerd asked, immediately thinking that was a dumb question.

"Of course we were," Cat said. "I mean, the last time we saw you at the party everything seemed as fine as ever. Then we heard about this."

Leah was nodding her head in agreement. "I think mostly we were surprised because no one knew you were going to do it."

An ironic laugh came from Gerd. "I wasn't even sure I was going to do it till Friday."

"So, spill it," Cat commanded. "What made you decide?"

"I've been thinking about something but I'm so confused. I change my mind ten times a day. I mean, I don't know. Maybe it just got planted in my head."

"What, Gerd?"

"I'm afraid to tell you," Gerd admitted after struggling wordlessly for a moment. "I wasn't as afraid to tell Richard but I knew I was breaking up with him. I still need your friendship and if you don't like this . . ."

"Don't like what?" Leah asked.

"Just tell us. You're driving us crazy," Cat said.

"All right. I'm not sure but . . . I think I could be gay."

It was very quiet for a moment. They were still looking at her, but Gerd was thinking that this was it. She'd just lost her two closest friends. The tears filling her eyes started to run down her cheeks. Now what the hell was she going to do?

Then Cat smiled as she shook her head. "Why do you think we'd have a problem with that?"

"Because that's not how we were raised. It's not acceptable. People who . . ."

"Gerd, there's nothing wrong with it at all." Cat hugged her from one side and Leah from the other.

"We had a talk on the way over here. We thought this might be what was going on."

"How could you guess this?"

"Well, silly girl," Cat broke into a grin, handing Gerd a Kleenex she'd dug from her pocket, "Richard was yelling at Max that she stole his fiancée, for one thing."

Gerd couldn't help laughing a little as she dabbed her face dry.

"And . . . we've talked about this before," Leah admitted.

"What do you mean exactly?"

"We thought you might be gay but you seemed so determined to go straight and then you got engaged."

"We're the biggest cowards on earth, Gerd," Leah told her as she put her arm around Gerd's shoulders and gave them a friendly squeeze. "We were afraid to say anything to you so we never brought it up."

"How many of my friends thought this?"

"Just us, as far as I know." Cat looked at Leah, who nodded. "I mean, it's just been the two of us talking about it."

"What makes you think I'm gay?"

Neither one of them said anything for a moment, then examples started to spill from both. "Things that most people look right over. Like, you tend to watch women and I don't think you even know you're doing it."

"When we talk about guys you never say as much as the rest of us but when we talk about women you gush."

"I don't gush."

"Yes, you do," they both said.

"And you pay much more attention to the actresses when we see movies. You're always talking about them. It's almost never men."

"Case in point, after you and Richard saw that play Max Ivers was in, it was like she was the only one in the whole show. You talked and talked about her."

"I did not."

"Yes, you did," Cat assured her. "You have a major crush on her. So, what's up with that anyway? If I were taking a wild guess I'd say she showed up at that party because you were there."

Gerd remembered how she'd felt as a kid when she was caught doing something wrong, so foolish and embarrassed and guilty because she hadn't gotten away with it. She tried to look down to hide her famous blush. Leah just laughed as she tilted Gerd's face up again. "C'mon, Princess Red Face. 'Fess up."

"Well, Max and I ended up talking in Richard's bedroom."

"Oooh."

"That was an accident. She didn't tell me to meet her in there or anything."

"Okay, keep going."

"We were talking about how I looked like I wanted out of there and then . . . she kissed me."

"Did you kiss her back?" Cat demanded excitedly.

"Yes. I didn't mean to. It just happened."

"And was it good?"

Gerd looked at the ceiling as she bit her lip. "It was a melt-your-knees kind of kiss." Finally, she'd said it out loud to someone. The relief she felt was incredible.

"Oh my." Cat fanned her face. "So what happened after that?"

"She invited me over to her apartment to talk after the party . . ."

"Her apartment. Oh my goodness."

"Yes, but nothing else happened, okay? She just asked me if I thought I might be gay and I said I wasn't sure. I told her I needed to think and she said she'd be willing to listen if I wanted to talk more. But I don't know what to say. I need time."

"So take it," Cat told her.

Gerd sighed. "I just don't think I can do this."

Leah squeezed her shoulders again. "Do you have feelings for her?"

"Yes."

"And does she have feelings for you?"

"She says she does."

"Gerd, it sounds like you're having trouble accepting what you already know. You like women."

"But what do I tell my family? I wasn't raised this way. They'll throw a fit."

"Gerd," Cat began, "why don't you cross that bridge when you come to it?"

"Meaning what?"

"You haven't even made up your mind about yourself yet, let alone gotten comfortable with a new identity. Just get out of your bedclothes first. Go to classes tomorrow. Make yourself some soup. You can deal with your family later. Let yourself have time."

"What if I still think I'm gay?"

"Then I highly recommend, even though she's very different from you and she hasn't passed our series of inspections yet, that you kiss Max again and see what happens."

Gerd blushed, of course.

Chapter Five

"Max, this is taking too long," Raney complained. She already had her bagel and cream cheese for lunch.

"Yeah," Gail agreed. "My coffee's getting cold."

Max made a face at them. "I doubt that, since I'm watching steam rise off of it."

Raney kept looking up to the next floor, waiting for her girlfriend, Constance, to come out of her sculpture class. "What did you order, anyway?"

"Pumpkin bread. He's looking to see if they have any more."

"Maybe they're growing it," Gail suggested, which brought a sizzling sound of appreciation from Raney and a scowl from Max.

"There's Constance," Raney announced. "We're going up to the tables."

"Fine, I never said you had to stay down here. I'll be up in a minute." Max turned to look at the drink machines. From the corner of her eye, she saw someone else come to the counter, hurriedly looking over the food and waiting for someone to take an order.

"Can I help you?" the guy working there asked the newcomer as he put two slices of pumpkin bread on the counter.

Hey, let me pay first, Max thought as she saw . . . Gerd. Gerd was the one ordering.

"I'll just take one of those salads." Gerd pointed to one. Then, reaching behind her, she pulled at the top of the zipper on her dress.

Max walked behind her and saw that the hook was about to pull loose. "Hi there. You look like you're a little the worse for wear."

"Oh my gosh, Max, hi," Gerd said, looking very startled. "I didn't even see you." She pulled at her dress again. "Something feels like it's coming loose back there."

"It is. Your hook's coming off and you're unzipping."

"Great. That's all I need. I have class in half an hour and I'm doing a presentation. I can't make it home to change." Gerd pushed her money across the counter.

"Well, unless you're into streaking I think you need a quick repair job."

"You don't have a needle and thread in your back pocket, do you?"

"Almost. We're next door to the theatre. I can take you to the costume shop and have you fixed up in no time."

"That's awfully nice of you, Max, but they're probably really busy."

"No, I meant I can do it. It'll only take a minute."

"Are you sure you don't mind?"

"If I did, I wouldn't have offered."

"Okay then, I accept."

Max started out of the food annex, thrilled that she'd talked Gerd into it, terrified that she'd sew it up wrong. Sewing had never been one of her talents.

"Hey, what about your pumpkin bread?" the guy behind the counter called.

Running back, Max said, "Can I pay you later?" He looked doubtful. "C'mon, I'm in here every day and there's a gorgeous woman waiting on me."

"All right, go on."

"Thanks," she said, running off without the bread, and forgetting to tell anyone she wasn't coming up to eat.

Following Max through a doorway in the theatre's basement, Gerd entered a room filled with industrial washers, dryers, and sinks. "This is where they do laundry and dye clothes," Max told her. "And if you look behind you, you'll see the shoe closet." Gerd looked through another doorway where rows upon rows of shoes lined the walls. Max pulled out a stool. "Here, sit down."

"Thanks, Max. Are you sure this is no trouble?" Gerd asked, setting her bag on the floor. "I mean, you left your bread and everything."

A sheepish look crossed Max's face immediately. "You weren't supposed to notice that."

"Sorry." Gerd looked down, hoping Max wouldn't see her grin.

"I'm going to get some thread. I'll be right back."

While she waited, Gerd tried to run through her presentation in her head. But between her nervousness that she'd screw up, her excitement over seeing Max again, and her stomach growling, she couldn't concentrate.

"Okay, we're in business," Max announced as she came back in.

"Great." Gerd bent her head so Max could get to the hook.

"I'm going to unzip this just a little."

Even with that warning, Gerd's breath caught when she felt Max pull her zipper down. It was such an intimate action, Max's fingers loosening her clothing. And the back of the neck was such a sensitive area. A blush rose to her face as she felt herself getting aroused.

"Are you okay?" Max asked her.

"I'm fine," Gerd said, trying to remember to breathe. "I'm just worried about this presentation I have to do. It's for my hardest class, management."

"When is this class?"

"In . . ." she looked at her watch, "five minutes."

"Well, I'll be done in one minute so quit worrying."

That was hard advice to take. It was against Gerd's nature. "You haven't run into Richard anymore, have you?"

"No, I haven't. Have you?"

"No. I got my stuff from his apartment and left my key when I knew he'd be gone. He calls every so often but I haven't changed my mind about us so I've been screening my calls. He tried to drop by one day but I pretended I wasn't home. I feel bad, dodging him like that. I mean, I don't dislike him, you know? It's not that. I just feel like right now I've said all I can say and if he's going to tell me I'm wrong I've got better ways to spend my time, you know?" Did whatever I just babbled out make sense? Gerd wondered.

"That makes sense to me."

"My family's driving me crazy," she said, enjoying every move Max's fingers made. The gentle tugs as she drew the needle through the material were making Gerd tingle to the tips of her toes. "My mother came right out and told me I'd made a mistake breaking off our engagement. Then she and my father drove down one weekend and tried to talk me into getting together with them and Richard, to figure out what went wrong. I think that's how she put it."

"You must feel tired of being pulled in opposite directions."

Gerd sighed as Max zipped her dress. "Yes, I am. That's a good way to put it."

"Well, your zipper's going to have an easier time of it. I'm all done."

"Max, how can I thank you, really? You have to tell me something." Gerd looked up at her, wishing Max would put her hands back on her shoulders.

"How about some coffee?"

"That sounds great. When can you get together?"

"Well, uh . . . could we do it tonight? The rest of my week is pretty busy."

"Tonight is fine with me," Gerd told her, slowly and reluctantly getting to her feet. "What time?"

"Is six okay? At the Golden Roast?"

"That's fine too."

"I'll see you then."

"Thank you so much, Max." Gerd started out with her mind now much more on Max than her presentation. Is it right to feel so attracted to this woman? Is this who I really am?

"Hey, Gerd, don't you want your salad?" Max asked.

Gerd laughed as she turned to get it. "I forgot I was even hungry." That told her a lot and scared her almost as much.

*   *   *

Sitting at a table in the Golden Roast, Max was so nervous she didn't think she'd even be able to drink anything. She tried some deep breathing exercises she'd learned in acting classes but they weren't working. What if my coffee doesn't stay down? What if I have to jump up midway through my cup and run to the restroom? Her stomach gurgled, as if to reinforce her thoughts.

Checking the front door for the hundredth time, Max wondered why being around Gerd made her so much more nervous than being around anyone else. She was a veteran of many dates, and her last girlfriend, Anna, had been a particular favorite of hers. But waiting on Anna had never made her this nervous. A little nervous, yes, but not this nervous. She forced herself to look at the people sitting at the bar instead of at the door.

The truth is, she admitted to herself, I'm more attracted to Gerd than I have been to anyone else. I'm also more afraid of screwing something up when I see her. What is it about her that gets to me so much?

Gerd came walking through the door and as their eyes met, Max felt a jolt like an electric shock. That's what it is, she realized. Even with all the things I described to Raney about the way she looks and smells and talks, the attraction is coming from this current I feel between us, this zing. I wonder if she feels it too. She does, doesn't she? She wanted to see me. What if this is just a polite gesture, though? I don't know what's going on in her head. Oh God, I'm nervous.

"Hi Max, I'm sorry I'm running a little late. You weren't waiting long, were you?"

"No, I've only been here a few minutes."

"Oh, good."

"How'd your presentation go?"

"You know, it was as smooth as silk. That's the best one I've ever done. Maybe it was because I didn't have so much time to think about it. I think I've been overthinking them until now."

"You think so?" Gerd smiled and, watching her eyes crinkle, Max felt as if she were floating right out of her body. "I see your dress stayed on," she said.

"Yes, it did. I can't thank you enough. So what would you like to have? My treat."

You. I'd like to have you, Max imagined saying. That made her chuckle out loud. "Sorry, I just thought of something. Let's go look at what's on the board."

Fortified by a latte, a mocha, and slices of chocolate maple cheesecake, they got into a discussion of the music they liked. Gerd preferred jazz vocalists, show tunes, and some contemporary pop.

"Celine Dion?" Max said, as if Gerd had admitted to liking the Chipmunks.

"Hey, she's got a great voice."

"Oh, I agree, she does. She's just too ballady for me."

"Uh-huh, and you never sing along with Karen Carpenter, right?"

"Hey, Karen Carpenter had a great voice."

"Ah-hah. Who else do you listen to?"

"Mary Chapin Carpenter, Eurythmics, Fleetwood Mac, Billie Holiday, Billy Idol . . ."

"That's quite a range."

"Yeah, I like a lot of different stuff. When I get home tonight I'm going to put on some Nanci Griffith. I've had one of her songs stuck in my head all day."

"Nanci Griffith? I've heard of her but I don't think I know any of her music."

"You're kidding. Nanci had albums before Celine Dion was even born."

"I really don't think I've heard her."

"Are you doing anything or could you come back to my place? You could hear some Nanci."

Gerd looked at her watch. "I've got a little time, I guess. I think I'd enjoy that."

"So do I."

Stretched out on Max's floor, with *Other Voices, Other Rooms* playing, Gerd was looking through a collection of photos thrown haphazardly in a small box. Max had been telling her about them when her phone rang. Some pictures were of Max, some were of family, and a ton were of her friends. There were people getting into costume, getting out of costume, working on costumes, working on sets, wearing headsets, etc.

Max came back in from her bedroom, where she'd gone to consult her calendar about dates for a rehearsal.

"You know, you should put some of these up," Gerd told her. "You could get a cork board or something."

"I've thought about it. I just never do it."

"You could get one really cheap at Target and then paint a border on it and stick these up with colored thumbtacks. Then you could write some captions to go with them."

Max stretched her arms. "That sounds like a lot of work."

"Oh no, it wouldn't take that long, really," Gerd assured her, easily picturing how it would look. "If you get a stencil you could make a pattern for the border in just a few minutes."

"You know, Gerd, that all sounds like a wonderful idea. But I think I'm more of a keeps-pictures-in-a-box person."

When am I going to learn? Gerd thought. I always want everyone to do things like I would. "I'm sorry, Max, I didn't mean to be pushy. Sometimes . . ."

"It's okay," Max interrupted. "I didn't think you were being pushy."

"Are you sure?"

Max punched her arm lightly. "Don't make me change my mind."

"Hey," Gerd said, punching her back, "I'm not the one who's afraid to use a box of thumbtacks."

"Oh yeah, well, I'm not the one who had to be sewed back into her dress today." Punch.

"You ran off and left your pumpkin bread." Punch.

"You were about to leave without your salad after your stomach was growling." Punch.

"You weren't supposed to hear my stomach, you sneak." Punch.

"Sneak? I'd have to be deaf to have missed that," Max managed to tell her through bursts of laughter. Gerd punched her. "It echoed off the walls." Gerd punched her again. "It was like a bomb going off." Gerd punched her harder. "It," Max started. "What is it?" Gerd was doubling over laughing.

"My hook just came loose," she said when she could finally get her breath.

Max started laughing too. "Are you sure?"

"Look and see."

Sure enough, there was the hook, loose, with the thread dangling from it. "Do you want me to sew it again?"

"No, I couldn't sit still long enough. I'm laughing too hard."

"I'm really sorry your hook broke."

"So am I."

"I mean, I'm sorry you broke your hook."

"I'm sorry about that too."

"Oh my God, Gerd. I'm so sorry." Max had tears in her eyes from laughing so hard. As she looked down at Gerd, she saw tears on her cheeks. "Here," she said, wiping Gerd's face with her fingers. Gerd suddenly stopped laughing and looked up at her with what Max could only call a misty-eyed expression. I can't help it, Max thought, kissing her.

Gerd kissed her back for a second, then pulled away. "Max, I'm sorry. Again. I want this. I just don't think I'm ready for it yet."

"Um, okay." Max pulled away, leaning against one of her chairs.

"I'm really sorry. I don't mean to be a tease. I've been thinking a lot about what we talked about, and I think I might be gay. I'm just not sure yet. But even if I am gay, I know I'm not ready to be, not mentally ready, I mean. The flesh is willing but the mind is weak, or something like that." Gerd started putting Max's pictures back in the box.

"I don't think your mind is weak," Max said. "I think you're a very strong person and you don't like to do things until you make up your mind. That's not a bad thing, Gerd. And no matter how attracted I am to you, I don't want you to do this if you're not sure about it."

"Max, you're a wonderful person. Thank you for being understanding and thank you for your perspective. It really helps."

"You're welcome. And Gerd, I think you're a wonderful person too."

Getting to her feet, Gerd suddenly felt drained. "I think I'd better go home now. But, Max, I swear you'll hear from me. I just need some more time."

"Take all the time you need. Thank you for the coffee." Max stood up.

"Thank you for fixing my dress." They both laughed. "And I really like Nanci Griffith. I'd like to hear some more sometime."

"You got it." Max walked Gerd to the door but they stayed far apart, afraid to touch each other now.

"Talk to you later," Gerd said, knowing she'd made the right decision but feeling lame anyway.

"Bye."

Feeling tired and frustrated, Max went back to sitting on the floor by her pictures. Why is this happening to me? she wondered. Why was it happening to Gerd? What else is going to happen? When? If?

Max's neck hurt and one side of her face felt hot as she finally opened her sleep-clogged eyes. Oh, no wonder. She was sitting in her Jeep with her head sliding off the headrest while the sunrise came through her windshield. For what felt like the hundredth time, she'd gone driving at night because she couldn't sleep.

April had hardly begun but it already felt like an endless succession of sleepless nights. No matter how she tried to tell herself that there was no point to it, she couldn't get Gerd out of her mind. Scenarios of seeing her again, kissing her again, making love with her popped into Max's head at far too many opportunities.

The fact was, she'd started to doubt that she'd hear from her again. A month had gone by and nothing. Of course, a month was nothing when you were weighing decisions that would change your entire life. But a month felt like eons when you were waiting to know if you had a chance to be with someone or not.

What if she doesn't call, Max thought, squinting as the bright, red ball of sun climbed higher over the Great Smoky Mountains. What if everything that's happened between us was just a big farce? What if . . . I'm going to go nuts, if I haven't already? I've got to find something else to do. She fumbled around in her glove compartment until she found her sunglasses, then decided to drive into Townsend for some breakfast. Thank God I don't have any early classes.

April was moving just as slowly for Gerd as it was for Max, and she wasn't sleeping any better. During the day she could distract herself with classes and studying–not that she had great concentration, but it was adequate. At night, though, question after question about herself, her identity, and what she wanted out of her life ran through her head. Unlike Max, she stayed in bed with her eyes wide open, her pillow and her body feeling equally knotted.

And more often than not, thoughts of Max ran through her head at night too. Never in her life had she felt this attracted to someone or even thought it was possible. It was easy to remember her gorgeous green eyes and her fingers stroking Gerd's face with a touch that made Gerd's hairs rise, followed by the touch of her lips. Heat rose in Gerd. When she remembered the feel of Max's tongue working its way forward she had to throw off the covers and sit up.

When she did get to sleep, her dreams thrust her into all sorts of situations with women. Many times, they were celebrities. She could barely believe most of the scenarios. What was her subconscious trying to do, besides drive her crazy?

At Cat's suggestion, she'd finally bought a dream journal. "Dreams aren't just there to amuse you, Gerd," Cat had said. "Your subconscious uses them to tell you things. If you write them down and go back over them, you'll probably figure it out."

One morning, after finally getting a decent night's sleep, Gerd fortified herself with a bowl of cereal and started reading through her journal. She wanted to count just how many dreams in, say, the last two weeks seemed to have something to do with lesbianism. Jodie Foster had pinned her on the floor of a gym in a movie they were filming. In an episode of *Cagney and Lacey*, she kept shooting at a man she couldn't hit. She was rolling around on the floor with Amy Ray of the Indigo Girls, while her mother and grandmother were sitting in the room. Her head was on the shoulder of Emily Saliers, the other Indigo Girl, at a concert where they were in the audience. A redheaded woman had appeared in her bed, treating her to such incredible sex she woke up in a puddle.

Wait a minute. Every dream in the last two weeks had something to do with lesbianism. She started flipping back to earlier weeks. The trend continued. When she finally realized she wasn't going to find anything but lesbian dreams, Gerd put her head back and laughed. You'll probably figure it out, Cat had said. Well, duh. "I'm a lesbian, no question," Gerd said, starting to laugh all over again. How much more blatant could my subconscious get? At least this laughing is helping me unwind. Thank God.

Now the real question is, can I live with this? Gerd got serious as she contemplated a whole new life. She was scared of changing her identity, scared of losing her friends, even more scared of losing her family, and she really didn't know how to be gay. She didn't know what gay people did. But she'd spent all this energy trying not to be gay, and where had it gotten her? Nowhere but alone and unhappy. Why not try improving things? Why not try living as a lesbian? What would happen?

Sunlight was streaming across her deck, through her sliding glass door into her dining room. As she sat, enjoying the warmth of the rays, Gerd didn't feel guilty, as she'd thought she would over her decision. What she felt instead was an overwhelming sense of relief, with maybe just a tinge of excitement, too.

After classes she'd hardly paid any attention to, Gerd started walking, not to her car, but up through the Fort toward the Mill House. She told herself that it wasn't polite to just drop in on people. Max might not even be home. She really needed more time to get comfortable with herself anyway. But all the while she was thinking, she kept right on walking up the hill, feeling better the closer she got to her destination.

This time, she arrived at Max's house from the front, where she couldn't see her Jeep. She started around the side, thinking she'd see if the Jeep was there before knocking. It was there. She took a deep breath. Just then, she jumped as an odd wooden thunk sounded behind her.

"Hey, stranger. What're you doing here?"

Turning around, she saw Max leaning out her window. A grin spread across Gerd's face. "I was just wondering if you were home."

"Does this answer your question?"

"Yes, I think it does."

"I'll meet you at the door, unless you'd rather climb up my hair."

"Thanks, but I'll use the door."

When Max let her in, Gerd felt excited and frightened and relieved, all at the same time. It was the combination of being around Max again along with knowing what she'd come to tell her, she supposed. Max stood looking at her for a second, then grinned. "What is it?" Gerd asked.

"You look really happy. I like it."

"Thanks."

They both stood looking nervously at each other for a minute until Max finally said, "Do you want something to drink or eat or . . ."

"Something to drink would be good."

"Okay, what would you like?"

"What do you have?"

Opening the refrigerator, Max looked inside. "Let's see, water, Coke, tea, milk, pineapple juice . . ."

"Pineapple juice," Gerd said.

"Ice?"

"Yes, please."

"It's going to take a minute to pry it out."

"You don't have to go to any trouble."

"It's no trouble. Why don't you go on in the living room? I'll bring it to you."

"Okay," Gerd said as she started that way, almost tripping over a box that sat dangerously close to the doorway. It was still open at the top, filled with books and CDs. "Are you packing or just cleaning out in here?"

"Oh God, I'm sorry. I forgot all about the box." A moment later Max pushed the box to the side as she handed Gerd her juice. "I'm seeing if I can fit everything I need in two boxes. If I can I think I'm going to Alaska for the summer."

"Alaska," Gerd echoed weakly, trying not to strangle on her first swallow. "Why would you go up there?"

"To work in summer dinner theatre. Gail was telling me about it. She says they pay really well."

"Are you sure you want to go?" Gerd managed to ask, although she felt crushed. Why had she ever thought Max would be waiting for her the minute she'd finally made up her mind?

Max took a deep breath. "Look, what I'm about to say isn't

meant to be any kind of a . . . pressure tactic." She looked Gerd in the eyes. "I just want to tell you the truth, okay?"

"Okay," Gerd said, wondering if Max could hear her heart pounding.

"I can't stop thinking about you, Gerd, and since that isn't going anywhere, I'm thinking maybe I should. No one's ever gotten to me like this before. I thought I could handle it, but nothing I do is working. Maybe if there are thousands of miles between us I can finally get a decent night's sleep. I just don't know anymore." As she talked, Max had backed a few steps away. Now she was looking down with a tired, defeated expression.

"Max?"

"Yeah?" She looked up.

"I, um . . . I can't stop thinking about you either."

"You can't?"

"No. See, the thing is, I could really use your help with something."

"What's that?"

"Well, I'm a lesbian . . ." Gerd paused, thinking that was the first time she'd ever said it out loud–I am, instead of I think or I might be.

"And you haven't even been struck by lightning," Max cut in.

Gerd laughed. "That's exactly what I was thinking. Anyway, I just needed to hear it loud and clear from myself, you know? Hey, Gerd, you're a lesbian. And my dreams did the trick. In fact, I'll have to tell you about them. They're really funny. But you helped get things started when you asked if I thought I might be gay. Which brings me to where I am now. There's a problem. Well, actually, there are several problems but one of them is, I don't know how."

"Don't know how?" Max looked puzzled.

"I don't know how to be gay. I was hoping you could give me some pointers." Gerd looked down at the floor, knowing her face was quickly going red.

Max walked over and reached out, and for a minute Gerd

thought she was going to cup her breast. But she put her hand on Gerd's glass instead. "May I take this?"

"Sure."

After putting the glass on the coffee table, Max scooped Gerd into her arms and headed for the bedroom.

No one, including the football player she'd dated, had ever scooped Gerd up as if she were a heroine in a movie. "I don't have any major diseases," she blurted as they went through the doorway. "I can't prove it but it's true."

"I don't have any either," Max said, kissing her as she set her on the bed. She thrust some papers from her nightstand into Gerd's hands.

The top page was a report from a clinic. All the test results were negative. "Wow," Gerd said, thinking that was the dumbest response possible. Max dropped them on the floor while kissing her again.

"Max?" Gerd said, as Max began to unbutton one side of her jumper.

"Yes?" Max stopped, looking at her distractedly.

"I never really went all the way with Maggie."

"Gerd, you have great instincts. Don't worry about a thing. But I promise, you'll get lots of pointers, okay?"

"Okay."

With a little help from her, Max slid Gerd's jumper onto the floor. She kissed her eyes, her lips, her neck, then carefully unbuttoned her blouse. Gerd shrugged out of it, watching it go over the edge of the bed. Would Max take something off now? she wondered. But instead, Max took Gerd's bra off, then slid her damp panties off too. "Oooh, you're so beautiful," she said, pausing to admire Gerd from head to toe.

She began to stroke Gerd with the tips of her nails. The lighter the touch, the more arousing it felt, and Max spared no inch of her. Soon, Gerd was tingling all over. A smile lit her face as she shivered involuntarily. She let her eyes close.

After drinking in that sight for a moment, Max blew very gently across Gerd's breasts. "Oh God," Gerd murmured, as Max began to alternate between blowing and stroking. As she raised up, Max took her nipple between her lips, bathing it with her tongue. Gerd came, knowing that as much as she'd enjoyed making love with the men in her life, this woman was bringing it to a whole new level, even during the foreplay.

Max went on, moving down to tongue Gerd's thighs until her toes had curled so much she'd made indentations in the bed. Then, slowly working her way back up, she planted a kiss over Gerd's heart, lingering with her head resting on her breasts for a moment. Just when Gerd was beginning to wonder if Max would ever undress, she slipped off her clothes. Then she slid her arms under Gerd, pulling her tight against her while she looked her right in the eyes. Gerd gave Max a long kiss. "I want you in me," she said.

"You got it." Continuing to look her in the eyes, Max slid one hand down, knit her fingers together and slipped them inside Gerd very slowly. Gerd's eyes went wide. She clutched Max so tightly that she knew her nails were making marks. Max began to stroke her inside, and in return Gerd thrust her hips, adoring the sensation as Max's fingers went deeper and deeper. Feeling as if she would explode, Gerd came in what she thought was the most prolonged orgasm she'd ever had.

Her breath was shaky. Her muscles were still rocking. She opened her eyes, looking into Max's gorgeous green ones. "You know," she managed to say, "that was nothing like I'd imagined."

"No?"

"No. It was better." Max laughed as she brushed Gerd's hair back from her face. "Can we do it again?"

"You bet," Max said.

And they did.

Chapter Six

Raney lifted her nose from the arrangement of cut flowers on Max's table. Some of her blond hair hung on the petals. She pulled it free, still enjoying the scent of an orange flower she couldn't identify. "God, Max, these are gorgeous." A tag said they were from Crouch's Florist. The vase was much more ornate than the usual ones for roses on opening nights at the theatre. "This must be expensive."

"She sent the wind chime too," Max called from the bathroom.

Lying on the table behind the flowers was a beautiful wind chime. It was a crescent moon with hollow stars hanging from it. There was a ring in the center for the stars to sound against.

Max walked back into the kitchen as Raney brushed her hand across the stars, making the chimes ring. Breaking into a smile, Raney looked at the crescent moon tattooed on Max's arm. The yellow moon sat on a teal background with a magenta star on the tip. "I guess she liked your tattoo, huh?" Max raised her eyebrows. "This chime will be so nice on the porch. I'm surprised you haven't put it up already."

The teasing tone in Raney's voice had started already. "I just woke up right before you got here," Max said defensively. "Well, except for when the delivery guy came. C'mon, let's rehearse."

"No way, you tease! Not until you spill it. How was it getting a girl out of the closet and into your bed?"

"I didn't get her out of the closet."

"Oh?"

"She came."

Raney swatted Max on the arm. "Max Ivers, I want the scoop out of you. You're as giddy as it gets."

"Raney Marie, you know how much I hate the word giddy."

"Own your feelings, Maxine."

"Okay, I am. I'm giddy. Are you satisfied?"

"You are, apparently." Max rolled her eyes. "Details, I need details."

"Get some lesbian erotica then."

"C'mon, Max. You're dying to tell, so just get over yourself."

For a moment Max paused, brushing her hand across the wind chime. She wanted to babble, she was in such a good mood, but she didn't want to give Raney the satisfaction. In her peripheral vision, she watched Raney grinning as she sounded the chime again. Oh, why try to hold out? She wanted to babble too much. "All right, all right. She came up here to see me. She walked right by the window when I was looking out. It was so weird, Rain. She was wearing this little jumper and a gauzy shirt. God, she looked good."

"Did you pull her in the window?"

"No, I let her in the door."

"And then?"

"I gave her some juice and we started talking about me going to Alaska."

"Did you tell her you couldn't stop thinking about her?"

"Yes."

"You dog."

"Hey, she said she couldn't stop thinking about me either."

"So you threw her on the floor?"

"No, she asked if I could give her some pointers."

"Pointers? That's a good one. I have to remember that. Then you threw her on the floor?"

"No, I carried her into my bedroom."

"You carried her? Oh, my." Raney fanned her face. "Well, was it what you wanted?"

A huge grin crossed Max's face. "Let's say I'm very glad Gerd got back on the bicycle of lesbian love."

"Pedal faster, Mary Ann," Raney crooned, doing her best impression of Tina Louise as she faked a swoon. "How does she make you feel, Max?"

"Raney . . . her kisses send zingers all the way to my toes. She fits against me perfectly and she cooked me one of the best breakfasts I've ever had. Pancakes to die for."

"Are you sure you want to rehearse tonight?"

"Yes, we need to," Max insisted.

"Are you going to stay in town now?"

"Yes, I am."

"Max," Raney paused for a second, "you're in love with her, aren't you?"

"It's a little too soon for the 'L' word, Rain." Max turned away, getting a glass of water. Besides being giddy, Max was also a little scared. What if she were falling in love with Gerd? She'd never fallen in love before. What if Gerd was falling for her? What if . . .

"Let's rehearse," she said, to keep her mind from going in any more circles.

The waitress set Gerd's and Cat's food down on the table. "If you need anything else just let me know."

"Thanks," Cat said.

Gerd just stared. She'd agreed last night to meet Cat at the Copper Cellar on "the strip," a street in the heart of campus with restaurants, fast food chains, bars, and stores on both sides. The strip was a daily haunt of students, professors, and the UT staff because you could grab a meal, a drink, and something new to wear and still make it to class or work on time. Normally, Gerd loved the spinach con queso dip that was one of the Cellar's appetizers. She'd really been looking forward to it before she got here. But now that it was in front of her, she didn't think she even wanted it.

"What's up with you?" Cat asked, after swallowing the first bite of her BLT. "You seem out of sorts."

Gerd brushed a chip through her dip idly. "I've only heard from Max once this week."

"Maybe she's been busy. Could you pass me that catsup?"

"I don't get it. I told her I wanted to make dinner for her. I mean, I can't just throw it together at the last minute. I thought I'd have heard from her again by now."

Cat smacked the bottom of the catsup bottle. "Maybe she's not used to having elaborate dinners made for her. Did she give you any idea when she might be free?"

"She said maybe tomorrow night or Sunday. She had plans tonight."

Cat drummed her fingers on the table. "She's playing at . . . Manhattan's? Yeah, that's right, Manhattan's. She and Raney."

The chip in Gerd's hand snapped in two. "Tonight?" Cat nodded. "I wonder why she didn't invite me? She just said she was busy."

"Look, if it was me in her shoes I would've invited you, but maybe she didn't think of it. I've got the impression, from what you've told me, that Max is very busy most of the time. Maybe she knew she had plans tonight but she didn't remember what they were."

"She's still had time to call me. She would've remembered what she was doing by today."

"She didn't think you'd want to go? I don't know. You've never been to see her play before. Does she know you'd be interested now?"

"She should. I made her breakfast. I sent her flowers and a wind chime. I even called her to make sure they got there and to ask her to dinner."

A laugh got away from Cat. "That's a lot of stuff, Gerd. But none of that has to do with her playing tonight. Maybe you overwhelmed her. Maybe she needs some time."

"No, I don't think she needs time." Gerd looked down at the table again. "I think I blew it."

"How would you have done that?"

"I don't know. That's what bugs me. I'm just afraid that's what happened." She looked back at Cat, who tried a reassuring smile.

"Gerd, I think you're making up things to worry about."

"Well, I wouldn't be doing this if she'd just call."

"Listen, sweetie, everybody's not wired the same, you know."

The waitress came back to their table. "Is everything all right?" She looked at Gerd's barely touched chips and dip.

No, Gerd thought. Everything's all wrong.

"Everything's fine, thanks," Cat said in a tone that told the waitress that what was wrong wasn't the food.

"Okay. I'll bring you another Coke," the waitress said.

"Well, if someone sent you gifts and then invited you to dinner, would you forget to invite her to your concert?" Gerd asked.

"No, I wouldn't. But that's me." Cat ate more fries. "Some people prioritize things differently from you and me. Maybe Max wants the time with you to be really special and she'll call when she has a free night just for you." Gerd didn't say anything. Cat nudged her leg. "Hmm?"

"Maybe she's ashamed to ask a straight girl out in public."

"I seriously doubt that. Besides, you're not straight, remember?" A smile crossed Gerd's face. "Listen, why don't you just go see them play tonight?"

"I can't go by myself."

"Well, you could, but . . ."

"I wouldn't have anyone to talk to and I'd look really pathetic."

"So?" Cat said. They both started laughing as the waitress brought the Coke. "Leah and I will go with you. It'll give us a chance to check things out for ourselves."

"Ha. It'll give you a chance to say you've got a date on a Friday night."

"I'm about to reach across this table and smack you, Gertrude."

"Do it and I'll turn your lap into a Coca-Cola swimming pool, Catherine."

They pretended to stare each other down for a minute, until Cat crossed her eyes. Gerd laughed. "Okay, I'll go. What time?"

"We'll pick you up about 8:30."

"Deal."

"Gerd, if I help you get laid again do you think you could help me? I need to find a boy who wants experience and no commitment so I can just throw him on the floor." Gerd's face turned crimson. "What?" Cat said. "Do you think I'm being too picky?"

Manhattan's was one of the choice places to play in the Old City. It had been there longer than some of the other clubs, was on one of the main corners, and had a reputation for booking talent, not just noise. A few years earlier, some area merchants had decided to undertake restoring Knoxville's run-down Old City. It had started slowly with a new club here and there. But in a short time, the clubs had developed good reputations for live local music and well-tended bars. People started to come there for the nightlife. Then more restaurants had opened to offer several different kinds of food–vegetarian, Japanese, Cajun and All-American within a few feet of each other instead of in different parts of the city. Shops had started opening next with the same idea, to specialize in selling exotic or elite or cheap items in one area. Now there were stores stocked with antiques, junk, jewelry, and thrift clothes too. There were clubs all over with busy bars, good music, and low cover charges. Plus, there were coffee houses for the literary, dance clubs for the headbangers, and street performers for those inclined to walk around.

"They're good," Leah half shouted to Gerd over the din in Manhattan's as Max and Raney finished a cover of "Crimson and Clover" and announced they were taking a break. Before that, while they were doing a new song called "Up in the Air," Max had looked right at Gerd during one line. Gerd felt as if she were going to float out of her chair.

"Yes, they are good," Gerd agreed. Even from the back of the room, where they were sitting because they hadn't realized what a following Alter Egos had, she still thought there was something electric about Max. It wasn't just that she had a beautiful voice or played guitar well or wrote insightful lyrics, although all of those things were true. The same things were true of Raney but Gerd didn't feel a zing to the tips of her toes when she looked at her. With Max, it was more the way she used her voice, the rich, casual, sexy tone that made Gerd want to cross her legs just hearing her introduce the next song. It was the way she strummed her guitar, as if it were something she loved to hold. It was the way she wore her torn jeans and sat on the stool barefoot, as if on her porch or onstage her demeanor wouldn't be any different. And, Gerd thought, it didn't hurt that she could catch glimpses of her tattoo while knowing firsthand what it was like to touch it.

"Gerd? Gerd?" Turning to Leah, Cat shook her head. "She's such a goner." Leah laughed, agreeing. "Gerd?"

A flick of something cold hit Gerd on the side of her face. She jerked around to see Cat dipping her fingers into her beer mug. "Don't go there twice, Catherine."

"Well, at least we finally got your attention."

"What do you want?" Out of the corner of her eye, Gerd could see that Max and Raney had stepped down off the stage.

"You never told us what Max said in her message."

"Yes, I did."

"No, you didn't. You've hardly said two words since we picked you up. You said, 'She left a message for me about tonight.' "

"That's eight words."

"Yeah, well, you've been on cloud nine ever since."

"No, Cat, I think our Gerd's just plain horny," Leah announced, setting her empty beer bottle on the table.

"Hey!" Gerd threw her napkin at Leah. "It's with good reason."

As she looked toward the stage, Cat nodded. "Agreed."

Unable to resist anymore, Gerd looked toward Max and Raney again. They were working both sides of the room, going to the tables, speaking to those they knew, shaking the hands of newcomers, giving the audience their personal attention. It was going to take a while for them to reach the back, Gerd thought. This whole side of the place was full. Manhattan's was split like a

V. You could hear the music from the other side, where the bar was, but you couldn't see the musicians.

She began to wonder how she was ever going to get to talk to Max. There were so many women vying for her attention. Some were trying to latch onto her when she came to their table. And some were getting up to hit on her. One woman put her arm around Max, saying something in her ear. Max smiled at her as she said something back, but Gerd noticed that she moved away, never putting her arm around the woman. In fact, Max was very gracious about all this attention but she was clearly networking as much as flirting. It made sense that she and Raney took the time to do this, Gerd thought. These were the people who paid for the new microphone stands they were using.

Still, Gerd craved some sort of recognition from Max. She wanted Max to come back to her table, leaving the crowd behind. The whole time they'd been playing, Gerd had been dying for Max to say the next song was for her, as she had for some other audience members. She had thought that might happen with "Crimson and Clover." Max did say they didn't play it often and that tonight was a special occasion. But she didn't get any more specific than that. Oh, who was she kidding? She obviously wasn't the only woman in this room who'd slept with Max. Why did she think she'd get special treatment after spending one night with her?

Eventually, Leah got another round of drinks for them. Gerd managed to discuss the artwork on display. Then, just as she looked back into the crowd, Raney walked by. Leah waved. She'd been in a women's studies class with Raney the semester before. Raney squinted for a second, then came over.

"Hi, it's Leah, right?"

"Right. And this is my friend Cat." Raney shook Cat's hand. "And you may have heard of Gerd."

A big grin lit up Raney's face as she reached for Gerd's hand. "You're the wind chime woman, right?"

The heat of one of her famous blushes rose from Gerd's face. "Yes, that's me."

"It's very nice to meet you."

"We're really enjoying your show," Leah told her.

"I'm glad you came. Listen, I hope you won't think I'm rude but I'm going to duck outside for a minute. It's so hot and smoky in here and we still have another set to play."

"I think that's a great idea," Leah said quickly. "Would you mind if I ducked out with you?"

"If we *both* ducked out with you," Cat added, as her eyes acknowledged someone coming to their table.

"Not at all," Raney said.

"Maybe I'll . . ." Gerd looked over her shoulder to see Max. She was smiling as she walked up. Gerd felt her own smile starting.

"I guess you got my message," Max said.

"Yes, I did."

"Do you mind if I sit down with you for a minute?"

"Please do." Gerd slid down so Max could have the end of the bench, all the while thinking that she hadn't sat down with anyone else. "Max, you're really talented. I'm so glad I get to hear you."

"Thanks. I'm glad you're here." Max eyed Gerd's sleeveless navy shirt and matching shorts. "You look very beautiful."

"Thank you."

"So tell me, is that dinner invitation still good?"

"It sure is. How about tomorrow night?"

"I can't wait."

Gerd was running late getting dinner ready. She wanted everything to be just right, but she was so flustered she doubted that anything was. She caught the edge of the lace tablecloth, trying to straighten it, and nearly pulled one of the plates onto the floor. Catching it with one hand, she noticed the flowers she'd bought weren't all the way down in the vase. When they wilted halfway through dinner, Max would take that as a sure sign that this was all wrong and say, "Well, Gerd, I really have to get going."

After giving her flowers some extra arranging, she hurried to the stove to see if the fettuccine was ready for the shrimp. Why isn't the oven hot? she wondered, as she stirred the noodles. Opening the door, Gerd realized there was no heat. The garlic bread sat in the pan waiting to bake, as frozen as it was when she put it in there a few minutes ago. "Damnit! I don't believe this." She turned the knob over to bake, noticing the temperature knob was set already.

There was a knock on her door. Gerd nearly dropped her spoon. Was that Max? Couldn't she have been just five minutes late? Maybe there was time to take a quick look in her bathroom mirror. No, Max was already standing out there waiting. But how do I look? Gerd grabbed a plate to check her reflection. She tried to get her hair to lie down. It poofed back out immediately. There was another knock on her door. Giving up on her appearance, Gerd went to greet her guest.

Max was standing there, wearing shorts, a dark green pocket T-shirt, and thong sandals. Gerd's immediate thought was that she'd over-dressed. She had on jeans but with a dressy blouse and flats. Casual, she told herself. You should take this more casually. Max is a casual person. Oh well, it was too late to change now. "Hi. Come in. Did you have any trouble finding me?"

"Not at all." Max pulled a bunch of red roses from behind her back.

"Oh, they're beautiful, Max. I love this shade of red. Thank you." Max gave her a quick kiss, but it still made Gerd feel lightheaded. She went to the table, starting to put the roses in with the other flowers.

"Oops. I guess you didn't need two centerpieces."

"Don't be silly," Gerd said as she arranged them. "Look how nice the roses and the carnations and the daisies all look together."

Max smiled when Gerd stepped back from the table. "You're right. They're nice together."

"Would you like a tour of my place, since this is your first time here?"

"Sure."

Gerd's kitchen had a white floor and dark brown cabinets. Clear glass canisters filled with everything from spaghetti to black beans to oatmeal were lined up on the counters. A rack of spoons, spatulas, and strainers hung over the stove. "I added this wallpaper to make things look a little more homey," Gerd explained as she pointed to the ceiling border with colorful fruits between rows of navy stripes.

"It's a nice touch. I've never attempted wallpaper."

The table Gerd had set was large enough for four. She'd covered the dark wood with two white tablecloths, a solid one underneath one with an eyelet pattern. "Is this china?" Max asked, looking at one of the plates. They were ivory-colored with thin gold bands around the edges.

"Yes, it's some of my grandmother's. She gave it to me when I moved down here."

"I'm still using my mom's beat-up dishes from when I was a kid," Max said, following Gerd into the living room. It was filled with a matching dark green sofa, a loveseat, and an armchair that all had matching beige and burgundy pillows. "It's so . . ." Max searched for the right word.

"Furnished," Gerd said. "It seems odd to me sometimes. I mean, I'm in college. I'm not supposed to have nice things yet. I'm supposed to have . . ."

"Bright orange and yellow cabinets." They both laughed.

"Oh, I hope you don't think I was putting your stuff down when I said mine is nice," Gerd apologized. "That's not what I meant at all."

"That's not how I took it," Max assured her. "Don't worry." As she turned to look out the sliding glass doors, Gerd heard Max's breath catch. "Oh, you've got a beautiful view. Can we go out on your deck?"

"Of course." As they walked across to the railing, Gerd drew in a deep breath of the spring air. The rolling mountains that rose before them were just starting to be covered with many shades of green leaves. Later in the summer, when the humidity felt like a swimming pool, the air was so hazy you could barely see an outline of the Appalachians from any view in Knoxville. But now, they were the most discernible features of the landscape. "This is one of the reasons I wanted this apartment," Gerd said. "I'm a sucker for a beautiful view."

"Me too." Max turned, bringing herself to look directly into Gerd's incredibly blue eyes as her heart began to pound harder. Just then, the timer on the stove rang.

"That's the bread. Are you ready to eat?"

"I'm starving." Taking a deep breath, Max savored the smell of the garlic. It must have been some sort of frozen or refrigerated bread, she thought, watching Gerd start to slide it out of a bag.

"Ow!" Gerd had grabbed the bread with her mittless hand when it got stuck. She dropped it, rushing to the sink and running cold water on her fingers.

Wondering how best to help, Max walked over beside her. "It's not too bad, I hope."

"No, it just stings. I can't believe I did that, how silly."

Going with a gut instinct, Max put her hands on Gerd's shoulders. "Why don't you come over here and sit down? You cooked the dinner. Let me serve it."

"But I . . . I mean, you don't have to do that. That's my job."

"Job?"

"As the hostess."

"Well, hostess, you seem a little flustered, if you don't mind my saying so. Just sit down and relax. I think I can handle getting the pasta on the plates." I hope I can, Max thought, walking Gerd to her chair. She took her plate back to the stove.

But first things first. Glancing in a couple of cabinets, Max selected a small glass. Filling it with some ice and water, she set it by Gerd's silverware. "If you want to put your fingers in that, it'll help take the sting out."

"Thanks," Gerd said, looking up at her with that grin that made her eyes crinkle. The effect left Max weak-kneed, but she forced herself back to the stove, loading Gerd's plate with shrimp fettuccine and two slices of bread.

"A toast," she said, raising her glass after getting her own plate. Gerd raised her glass as well. "To a beautiful view." God, that sounded sappy, Max thought as they clinked their glasses. "Let's eat." A few minutes later, Max finally stopped chewing long enough to compliment the cook. "Gerd, this is delicious."

"I like to vary the texture of my food sometimes, so that's why I added the shrimp."

"It's a great combination. I wish you'd have let me bring the bread or something."

"I wanted to treat you. You can pitch in the next time."

"Okay." Max sipped some wine.

"Hey, you know something? The night we came to see *Present Laughter*, Richard told me you want to go to Yale for grad school. Is that true?"

"Yes, it is. I want to go to the Yale School of Drama. It's one of the best."

"I just can't believe what a coincidence this is."

"What?"

"I want to go there for grad school too. They have such a fantastic business school. I want to get my MBA."

Max was so amazed she stopped eating for a moment. What are the chances, she wondered, that this woman and I are headed in the same direction? "Life certainly is funny sometimes."

"You can say that again," Gerd said, rolling her noodles around her fork. "Hey, you know something else? I hardly know anything about you, except for that."

"What would you like to know, Madam?"

"Oh, mundane things to start with, I guess. Like where are you from?"

"One of the Tri-Cities."

"Aren't they on the Virginia border? I grew up in Richmond."

"Well, then, I grew up on your border." Max smiled at her and Gerd smiled back. "In Kingsport, to be specific."

"Is your family still there?"

"My mom is. She and my dad divorced and we haven't heard from him in years. I have an older sister who's married and lives in Nashville. Her name's Abbie. She's a PR mogul."

"Are you close to your family, Max?"

"Hmm, that's a hard question to answer. I am and I'm not. My mother and I talk pretty often, but I leave a lot out of our conversations. I guess you'd say I tell her what she wants to hear."

"Does she know you're gay?"

"Yes, she does. I told her one night when she said that I never let her in on my life."

"How did she react?"

"I don't think she was surprised, but at the same time, I think she had been hoping she was wrong."

"What about your sister? Do you get along with her?"

"Most of the time. We really like each other, but we're very different. She's the driven one and I'm the artist. Sometimes I think she worries that I'm nuts doing theatre, playing in clubs, being a lesbian." They both laughed. "But we're still close. She looks out for me."

"It's a common trait among older siblings. I look out for my younger brother, Gerald."

"Where's he?"

"He's still in Richmond with my parents. He's a junior in high school. Well, actually I guess he's almost a senior. Oh God."

Max laughed again. "Are you close to them?"

"Well, we talk twice a week like clockwork. But I think you hit the nail on the head a minute ago. There's a lot I leave out of our conversations, especially lately."

Max twirled her fettuccine in silence for a moment. "I want to ask you something, Gerd, but I don't want to offend you."

"I don't think you will. What is it?"

"You're a Virginia blue blood, aren't you?"

Gerd smirked. "What gave it away?"

"Um, let's see, your furniture, your manners, your china." Max paused, reflecting on what she'd just said. "I'm not criticizing. I'm just saying your background shows, maybe to me more than to some other people. It's very different from the way I grew up, which was strictly lower-middle class. But I'm not putting that down either."

Gerd nodded as she dabbed her mouth with her napkin. "You're right on target with my background. I'm from old Richmond blue bloods. Doctors and lawyers and stock brokers and such." She looked off for a moment. "They go to church every Sunday. The men play golf on the weekends. The women play bridge and serve these immaculate dinners on their great-grandmother's china."

"I bet you have horse trophies in your old room at home," Max said teasingly. "You're painting such a clear picture for me. Am I right?"

Gerd laughed as her face got a little red. "Yes, I have horse trophies. God, I hadn't thought about them in ages." She laughed again. "Charlie Brown, that was my horse's name. My best friend, Maggie, she's the one who fooled around with me, she had a horse named Peanuts. We used to love to go riding together."

It was quiet for a moment as they both sensed some heaviness working into the conversation. "Your family's going to have a problem with your being gay, aren't they?" Max finally asked.

Gerd swallowed some wine before she nodded. "Yes, they are. They're still upset about Richard so I'm not planning on telling them anytime soon. If ever. I just can't even imagine what they'd think or what they'd have to say."

"If you want my advice . . ."

"I'd really like that."

"Get comfortable with yourself first. Then you can think about whether you want to make them uncomfortable."

What a nice way of putting it, Gerd thought. "That sounds good to me."

"I think we ought to go for a lighter topic now. If you're from Virginia, why are you going to school in Tennessee?"

Gerd's smile returned. "I was in love, I thought, with a football player named Andy Dover."

"I see."

"And you know any serious boy . . ."

"Would come to Tennessee to play for the Vols," Max said, through a mouthful of fettuccine.

"That's right. We broke up at the end of freshman year and by that time I had taken to Knoxville and I didn't want to lose any credits in a transfer so I stayed."

"I'm glad you did," Max told her, running her foot along Gerd's leg.

"So am I," Gerd said. Her incredibly blue eyes crinkled in another smile.

After helping load the dishwasher, Max came back from the bathroom to find Gerd hopping around the kitchen holding her foot.

"What's the matter?" Max asked, unable to keep from laughing. Gerd looked as if she were doing half of a Laurel and Hardy routine.

"I've got a cramp in my foot. Ow! There it goes again."

I can help with this, Max thought. She shut the dishwasher and scooped Gerd up in her arms.

"Are you going to give me more pointers?"

"Yes, they'll distract you from the pain," Max said, carrying her to the couch. Sitting down, she put Gerd's foot in her lap and pulled off her shoe. The muscle spasmed, making Gerd's foot contract, while she sucked her breath in painfully. Max began to rub Gerd's foot with her warm hands. "Oh," Gerd moaned after a moment.

"Is that helping?"

"Definitely. Normally, my foot's really ticklish."

That's a good thing to remember for later, Max thought. "Should I do something else then?"

"No, no, that feels really good." Max went on rubbing her foot until the muscle relaxed completely. Gerd's eyes were closed. Max listened to the sound of her breathing growing steadier and deeper as she relaxed too. "I'm so glad you're here," Gerd murmured.

"So am I," Max agreed. She shifted until she could brush her lips along the top of Gerd's foot. Gerd made a small sound of surprise. Max planted kisses all the way down to her toes. Then, looking up, she saw Gerd gazing at her with misty eyes as her hands curled against the cushions. Leaning back down, Max breathed on her toes, then ran her tongue along them, taking one into her mouth. In response, Gerd moaned and shifted closer to her. Max kept on sucking, moving from toe to toe until she felt Gerd's fingers under her chin. She looked up.

"Kiss me," Gerd murmured.

"Where?" Max teased, lightly kissing her fingers.

"Not on my foot. I'm already lying in a puddle."

"I believe I need to confirm that first," Max said, unzipping Gerd's jeans. She slid her hands inside, around Gerd's hips, and pushed her jeans down. Gerd kicked them the rest of the way onto the floor. Max put her hands on Gerd's damp panties. "Yes, I'm afraid these will have to come off too." This time she slid her hands around Gerd's bare skin. Gerd sighed as she gently pulled the panties off. "Kiss you, did you say?" She undid Gerd's blouse and bra, which Gerd quickly shrugged off, and pushed her down onto the pillows.

"Oh my God," Gerd blurted as Max began to kiss her inner thighs, thoroughly enjoying the taste of this woman's skin along with the growing feeling of wetness between her own legs. She tongued Gerd's thighs until her hips began thrusting in rhythm. Max took the plunge, as she liked to call it, sliding her tongue in and out of Gerd, feeling her muscles quiver more and more in response.

Gerd came twice in a row before she was finally still. Max put her head on Gerd's belly, listening to the sounds of their raspy breathing. "I've never enjoyed doing that so much."

After a moment, Gerd stroked Max's face with her hand. "Come here."

Max did. Gerd lifted Max's T-shirt over her head. Then she pulled Max against her until their breasts were touching, kissing her as their tongues twined together. She and Max pulled her shorts off together. Gerd sank onto the pillows again, wrapping her legs around Max's, holding her close for a moment. Max sensed that Gerd was getting ready to do something, so she forced herself to be still. It wasn't long until Gerd slid her hands under Max's butt and then slipped her fingers into Max from behind. Max knew she was partly excited because Gerd had never done this to a woman before. But she was just as excited because those were Gerd's fingers inside her, stroking her, teasing her, going deeper.

Max moaned, driving her tongue even further into Gerd's mouth. She wanted to wait, to prolong everything, but she only lasted a few minutes until she came for Gerd the very first time.

"Was that good?" Gerd murmured against Max's lips.

"So good, Gertrude. You are divine."

"If you'd show me some pointers, I'd be willing to try it again."

"You're on."

The phone rang. It took a moment for Gerd to figure out which arm was free to get it. As she picked up the receiver by her bed, she noticed Max hadn't let go of her, hadn't even moved, in fact. The men she'd slept with hadn't held her very often once they were sleeping. They were more likely to just put a leg or arm across her. Richard had held her occasionally, but he always let go if the phone rang. She hated that. She had a hard enough time staying warm when she was sleeping, always wearing a nightshirt at least. Max was like a heater. Both times she'd slept with her Gerd hadn't worn a stitch of clothing and she woke up so cozy she didn't even miss it. "Hello?"

"Hey G, did I wake you?" her brother's voice asked.

"Yes G, you did. What's up?"

"I'm sorry, Gerd. I'll call you back tomorrow."

"No, what is it? I'm awake now."

"Mom and Dad don't want me to go to the beach for spring break."

"Don't want you to or won't let you?"

"Well, okay, they said I can't."

"Why not?"

"Because they found out Roddy got arrested for DUI."

"So don't go with Roddy, then."

"But he's the one with the reservations."

"Sounds like you're screwed to me, little brother G."

"Man, this break is going to suck."

"That's too bad." Gerd paused for a moment, knowing what he wanted, wondering if it were such a good idea. Well, she and Max weren't living together, or even getting to see a lot of each other for that matter, so maybe it wouldn't be so hard to keep the truth from him. "When is this break?"

"Next week."

"Next week?" That was typical Gerald, short notice. Gerd sighed, wishing she'd had more time to prepare. "Okay, why don't you come visit me instead?"

"Are you sure you don't mind?"

"It's okay by me, G. Run it by them tomorrow and give me a call."

"I will. Thanks, Gerd. Good night."

"Good night."

Gerd hung up the phone, waiting for Max to ask her if that was her little brother who might be visiting. But Max only stirred long enough to pull her tighter, brushing her lips to the top of Gerd's head. Maybe she hadn't even heard.

Chapter Seven

"Two weeks, good God. Are you sure? All right, fine, whatever. You'll call then? I promise, you're not as sorry as I am." Max clicked off her cordless phone. Constance was flipping through one of the magazines on the coffee table. Raney was looking through the latest stack of used CDs Max had bought. Neither of them was reacting to her trauma in the least. "Two weeks for the new part to come in for this washer. Can you believe that?" She kicked the paneled door of the utility closet behind her. "Ow!"

"Don't enter a crisis state, Max," Constance told her. "It's not like there aren't plenty of laundromats around here." She flipped to the next page in the magazine. "There's a couple in here who got married with their bridesmaids dressed up like swans. Can you believe that?"

"What's the matter, Max?" Raney teased. "Don't you save your quarters anymore? Have you gotten spoiled with a washer of your very own?"

"Yes, I have," Max whined. "I got so tired of piling my car full, losing money because the washers were broken, and ending up with pink underwear because someone used dye, and no matter where I went, the place always smelled funny."

"God, I forgot all about the pink underwear incident. I had to dress beside you and your pink underwear for the whole run of *Christmas Carol*," Raney said.

"Was it as good for you as it was for me?" Max muttered, still crabby.

"It sounds like you need to visit someone where you can do laundry. Now, I bet you don't want to drive all the way home to Mom, so . . . what about Gerd? Does she have a washer and dryer?" Raney smirked as she looked over at Constance, who smirked back. Both of them liked to needle Max, especially lately.

Max tried to ignore them. "Yes, she does, but I can't go over there. Her brother's visiting this week."

Constance looked over her glasses at Max. "Does he disallow doing laundry in his presence?" She balanced her apple core very carefully until it stood on a coaster. "If we were in a major city I could sell this little display for hundreds of dollars."

"Look, it's just that Gerd's family is very straight-laced and she's not ready to tell them what's going on yet so we agreed it's better not to get together again until he's gone."

"I see." Constance looked at Max again. "And is it better, avoiding temptation, as it were?"

"I'm doing fine here," Max assured them, too quickly.

Constance and Raney both burst out laughing. "You can't even wash your clothes," Raney teased her.

"Both of you can stuff it." Max started throwing dirty laundry at them.

"Max," Constance growled as her apple core tumbled off the table, "you're wrecking my art." A shirt draped her face. She snatched it. "This is the extreme of airing your dirty laundry."

"Truce!" Raney yelled, catching a pair of jeans. "Are we going to see a movie or not?"

Max dropped her dirty sock back on the laundry pile. "Yes, let's go before I get down to the underwear. Has anyone seen my shoes?"

There was a knock on the door, though Gerd barely heard it in the kitchen. Gerald had the TV turned up as though he was hard of hearing. Who could be here? she wondered. "Gerald, could you get that?"

"Someone's at your door, Gerd."

He wasn't even paying attention to her. She dried her hands on her dishtowel, rounded the corner and noticed that Gerald had . . . "A beer? What're you doing drinking a beer?"

"It was in the refrigerator," he said, as though that automatically made him legal.

"That doesn't mean you can have it. It's a beer."

"So?"

There was the distinct sound of someone dropping something against the door outside, along with a muffled "Shit!" Whoever it was had certainly heard them.

Gerald looked at Gerd patiently. "Aren't you going to see who's here?"

Gerd opened the door to find Max picking up a laundry bag that had rolled off a full laundry basket. "Hi," Gerd said, thinking she sounded too surprised. But she was surprised.

"Hi." Max stood. She was wearing cut-off denim shorts, a form-fitting T-shirt and her thong sandals again.

God, she looks good, Gerd thought. Why does she have to look so good right now?

"I thought you told me to bring my laundry over today," Max said.

"Did I? I thought I said tomorrow."

"Did you?"

"I don't know." Max backed up a step as if she were about to leave. "This is silly," Gerd blurted. "Come in."

Max picked up her laundry. "Are you sure?" she mouthed, walking by Gerd.

Gerd nodded distinctly, touching Max's arm as she shut the door. "Max, this is my brother, Gerald."

Max saw a young guy sitting on the couch. He looked at her, under the brim of his baseball cap, with the same blue eyes as Gerd's. In fact, now she could see he had nearly the same color blond hair as Gerd did too. His was shorter, though. It was probably wavy. He was handsome.

As he stood up, he looked surprised that Max was almost his height. "Nice to meet you." He held out his hand.

Max shook it, wondering what he'd think if he knew that she'd been making love with Gerd right where he'd been sitting. "Nice to meet you too."

"I was just picking out some vegetables for supper," Gerd said. "I'm making stir-fry. Can you stay?"

Max made what Gerd thought must be an "I hate vegetables" face. "No thanks. I have to leave as soon as this stuff gets dry. We've got a rehearsal tonight."

"Okay. I'll show you how to start the washer." They went down the hallway to the utility room. Gerald turned the TV up again. "Did I really tell you today?" Gerd asked, lifting the washer lid.

"I don't know. I'm pretty absentminded." Max's laundry bag swung from one hand. "Do you want me to go?"

"No, for all I know I may have said today. Besides, there's no reason for us to be this worried. I'm sorry I'm so flustered every time you come over. Are you doing whites first?"

"Yeah, whites. It's okay that you're flustered. I think I understand. You've made some big changes in your life and the ground under your feet still feels shaky." Max started dumping the whites in the washer.

Max was very close to touching Gerd and Gerd found herself almost wishing she would. Ridiculous scenarios of grabbing each other right here in the laundry room just as Gerald started down the hall to the bathroom amused her for a minute. "Shaky ground is certainly part of it," Gerd admitted. "Plus, I've been trying to entertain Gerald this week, which is fun and a major pain at the same time. He's going to turn eighteen in just a few months and Mom and Dad strictly forbid most of what he wants to do. I've been torn between playing the cool sister and the responsible daughter, you know?"

"I do know, believe me. I put my sister through the same stuff. When does he go back?"

"Tomorrow." Gerd started the water running. Max gave her a seductive smile for a moment before they went back down the hall. "Would you like a beer, Max? Gerald's indulging himself a few years short of the mark."

"Yeah, I would like one, thanks." Max turned to look at the television where the Pittsburgh Steelers were executing a beautiful pass. "Bradshaw to Lynn Swann, what a pair. Is this the retrospective ESPN put together? I missed it last fall."

"Yeah, it is." Gerald looked a bit surprised to be having this conversation, but he kept talking. "I missed it too. This is the 'Great Passers' part. Montana's on next."

"Montana to Jerry Rice, give them six."

An odd look came across Gerald's face. "How do you know about football?"

"I played it until I fell in love with the theatre. Don't look so surprised, bud. Women like football too."

"I guess I just never met any that did before." Gerd lingered getting Max's beer, laughing at the exchange she was overhearing.

"Well, now you have. I was one hell of a, heck of a, quarterback." Gerald laughed in disbelief. "I'm serious. I was the best pass interceptor on the block, too. And every Sunday afternoon I was glued to the tube."

Now he was getting into the discussion. "Who's your favorite pro team?"

And Max was getting more animated. "In the '70s it was the Steelers . . ."

"You really oughta stay and eat with us, Max," Gerald was saying. "Gerd makes a mean stir-fry."

Max added a folded towel to the stack in her basket. "I wish I could, but tonight we're starting rehearsals for a show I'm in."

"It's not the summer musical already, is it?" Gerd asked from the kitchen.

"No, that's the next show. Right now we're doing a quick production of *Oh Coward* in the Lab Theatre. There's not much to it. It's a musical review, kind of a bio of Noel Coward. It's mostly just songs with a five-piece orchestra. But that's the second show we've done this year that's by Noel Coward. You'd think he was still alive."

Max put her laundry bag on top of her basket. "Well, I've got to get going. Has anyone seen my shoes?"

Gerd laughed. "Do you ever wear your shoes inside?"

"Not if I can help it."

Gerald saw them by the living room chair and handed them to her. "It was really nice meeting you, Max. Next time I'm here you'll have to come back over so we can watch a game."

"I'll take you up on that, Gerald."

He went down the hall into the bathroom. Gerd looked after him with a grin. "He can't hold his beer yet."

A grin spread across Max's face too. As she went to the door, Gerd reached around her to open it. "Take care, Max."

"I'll call you soon."

Max looked at Gerd as though she wasn't sure what to do for a moment, then bent down to kiss her. Gerd meant to cut it short, fearing Gerald would catch them, but it became an extended touching of tongues instead. Finally, they pulled apart. Max backed quickly out the door.

Gerd slid the deadbolt into place and turned around to find Gerald standing in the living room with a shocked look on his face. Oh shit. Her heart started to pound very hard. "You saw me kiss her, didn't you?" she asked shakily.

For a moment he just nodded, then he swallowed hard. "I'm sorry, G. I didn't mean to."

"I know you didn't. I'm not mad at you, but we need to talk." Gerd wanted to run out the door, chase down Max's Jeep, jump in and never come back. I can't do this. I can't do this, she thought. But I have to do this. There's no going back now.

Sitting down on the couch, Gerd patted the cushion beside her. "C'mon, G."

Gerald looked very unsure of himself as he sat. "Is that why you gave Richard the ring back? Because of Max?"

"Yes, it is. Or, I mean, no, it's not because of Max." She drew a deep breath. Other people had gotten through this. So could she. "I gave Richard the ring back because I realized I'm gay, Gerald, and I always have been. Does that surprise you?"

"Yeah."

"Well, it surprised me too, kind of, but it's the truth." She paused again. "I don't know what you think of gay people."

Looking down, he said, "I haven't thought much about them really."

"Well, they may be different from you in some pretty fundamental ways, but they still like to sit down and watch football games." Gerd took his hands. "Do you know what I mean?" He shook his head. "They, I mean we, I need to start saying we, still have things in common with you even though th . . . we're different. Mom and Dad gave me the impression growing up that there's something wrong with gay people, and I believed that all these years. But just about a month ago, I finally accepted the fact that I'm gay. And what's important for you to understand, Gerald, is that there's nothing wrong with me because I'm gay. I was born this way and it's just fine. You may find that hard to believe, but it's the truth. I've always been gay. Maybe I would've realized it a long time ago if I hadn't had such a problem with it myself."

She stopped, waiting for him to say something. "Okay," he told her after a moment.

"I didn't want to be a lesbian. I thought if I didn't live my life like one, those feelings would go away, but then I met Max and I realized that wasn't going to work." Gerd paused, giving that a moment to sink in for both of them. "I guess the main thing I want you to know is this: gay people deserve your respect even if you don't understand why we're gay."

Gerald swallowed hard as he looked her in the eyes. "I would never disrespect you, Gerd."

Tears came to her eyes. She put her arms around him. "Thank you, G. That means more to me than you'll ever know." She held him for a moment, then pulled back to wipe her eyes. "I do want to ask you not to say anything to Mom and Dad about this."

"They'll throw a fit," Gerald said, shaking his head at the thought.

"I know. I've been thinking about that, believe me. I do want to tell them at some point, but I'm not ready yet, and I want it to come from me, okay?"

"Okay, Gerd. I won't say anything. I promise."

"Thank you."

"Um." Gerald looked down again as his face started to get a little red. "So, is Max your girlfriend?"

"Yes, she is," Gerd said, feeling proud to confirm that.

"You know what?" he asked, grinning at her.

"What?"

"It's weird but I like her more than any of your boyfriends, even the football player."

"I like her more than any of my boyfriends, too, G. Maybe it's not so weird after all."

Chapter Eight

"Are you hungry?" Max asked when Gerd was over the next week.

"I'm starving. What about you?"

"Ditto. Let's walk down to the Falafel Hut."

The Falafel Hut was a Middle Eastern restaurant specializing in hummus, baba ghannouj, tabbouleh, baklava, and a long list of beers. Anyone who lived in Fort Sanders, a neighborhood including housing from condos to apartment complexes to divided Victorian houses to condemned houses, might be eating at the Hut on a given night.

Thanks to the food and that diverse gathering of eaters, the Hut was one of Max's favorite restaurants. She could go there with a crowd of English major intellectuals and exchange wisdom, wind down with the cast after a show, or go alone and strum her guitar. Plus, she could take her shoes off and never get a dirty look from the staff.

As Max held the door open, Gerd waved at two women who were finishing their meal. The women looked at her as if she'd just flashed them. One gave her a half wave while the other leaned across the table, saying something as she eyed Gerd and Max with a cross between curiosity and disgust.

"Who're they?" Max asked. Gerd stood still, staring at the two women. Max steered her to a table on the other side of the restaurant.

There was a slightly stunned expression on Gerd's face as she sat down. "That's Katrina Jenkins and Sharon Armstrong. They talked about helping Cat and Leah throw a bridal shower for me." She let out a shaky breath as a waiter set down menus and water. Trying to distract herself, she studied her menu for a minute before she looked back at Katrina and Sharon's table. They were looking right at her, talking with their heads close together. What were they saying? she wondered. Nothing very complimentary, that was obvious. No wonder she hadn't heard from them since she'd broken off her engagement. She looked away.

Max saw the tears in her eyes. "Hey, I know this must be hard," she said, putting her hand on Gerd's, "but the best way to take the sting out of it is to go right on with what you were doing."

"I'm not sure I'm ready for this," Gerd admitted, squeezing Max's fingers. "But I guess it's now or never, because they're coming over here." And I'll be damned if I'll let them see me cry, she thought, quickly blinking back her tears.

"Gerd, my goodness, we were beginning to wonder about you," Katrina chided. "You've practically been in hiding since you broke poor Richard's heart."

"It would take more than me to do Richard in," Gerd said, feeling the subtle pressure of Max's hand giving hers an extra squeeze.

"Is this your new friend?" Sharon asked, looking down at Max with such a catty expression that Max felt like giving her a good smack. But she smiled politely instead.

"Max Ivers, this is Katrina Jenkins and Sharon Armstrong."

"It's nice to meet you," Sharon said, with her gaze locked on Max's and Gerd's hands.

"It's nice to meet you too," Max said, looking Sharon right in the eyes. Sharon looked away quickly, as if she were mortally offended. Looking over Sharon's shoulder, Max met Katrina's eyes as well.

Instead of looking away, Katrina stared right back, enjoying every minute of this. She almost seemed to be gloating. Max could bet she couldn't wait to get home, call her friends, and tell them about running into Gerd and her lesbian lover.

Gerd sat watching all this, wondering what she'd ever seen in these two women.

"Well, we'd better get going," Katrina said. "Don't keep your head buried in the sand too long, Gerd. You might just need to come up for air sometime." Sharon led the way to their hasty exit.

"That's just about the most insulting thing I've ever heard," Max snapped, the minute they were outside. "I'll go kill them for you, Gerd. It says right in the Bible, thou shalt not suffer a witch to live."

"No, honey, don't go kill them." Gerd drank some water and sat quietly for a moment. She felt numb. "Are you used to that, Max? People being so ugly to you? I mean, I've just never been through anything quite like that. I don't even know what to do."

"It doesn't happen to me very often, to tell you the truth. But when it does, I just try to ignore them or keep them from seeing how much they get to me. I usually can. This was quite a test, though. Anyway, you'll get more used to things like this."

"I'm not sure I want to be used to this."

"Gerd, I'm not saying that you should go around expecting it or take some kind of silly false pride in it, but sooner or later you'll have to face the facts. Some people are going to treat you ugly because they're ugly. They'll never see it that way, though. Not everybody sees being gay as something normal. Even you're still getting used to the idea."

"What if I can't get used to it? I mean, what if some part of me always holds out?"

"Baby steps, Gerd. Just take baby steps for now. I'll tell you a story that may help you. But I'll only do it over some food. My stomach's eating its way out of me."

Gerd managed to give Max one of her eye-crinkling grins. "Thank you for offering to kill them for me, honey. I can tell you care."

Max grinned back before she motioned to the waiter.

"When I was in fifth grade," Max began over a serving of pita bread and hummus, "I was part of this inseparable clique, part guys and part girls. It made me feel really special because we were all smart and funny and the way we hung around together made us seem cool, you know? We were kids that the other kids wanted to be around. Anyway, I had a crush on this girl named Katherine Kowalski who wasn't part of our group, but I didn't tell anyone because I knew that would put me out of the in crowd.

"Katherine liked me too. We would always flirt with each other when we thought no one was looking. One day we ran into each other at the Seven-Eleven. I used to go by there almost every day to buy cinnamon suckers, which I absolutely loved, and everybody in my class knew it. Anyway, when I saw Katherine that day she smiled at me and then she went up to the counter and bought some cinnamon suckers and motioned for me to follow her outside. We went behind the store and she gave them to me. I didn't know what to do because none of my friends had ever done something like that for me before. I looked down for a minute, and then when I got the courage to look up she kissed me.

"I thought I was going to have a heart attack and die, but it felt so good that I kissed her back. Then we got so carried away that we put our arms around each other and kept right on kissing. And then I heard people calling us names. Some of my friends were standing there looking at us with these horrified expressions and they were calling us lesbos and homos and faggots and I don't remember what else. Katherine and I ran off in opposite directions.

"The only consolation I had that night was thinking that at least she and I were in this together. I faked sickness the next day, but when I went back to school I found out we weren't in anything together. Katherine told everyone that I thought of the whole thing and grabbed her and forced her to kiss me and that she thought it was icky.

"In fact, my clique took her in and I ended up being totally shunned by them. They quit speaking to me unless it was to call me names, started all sorts of rumors about me, and even drew nasty pictures of me and circulated them. I was so ashamed I never told anyone, not even my mom or my teacher. Luckily, it was near the end of the school year so I didn't have to endure that treatment for long. And the next year we started middle school. Some of the rumors followed me but I made new friends." She grinned with what Gerd thought was a rare show from Max of false bravado. "The end."

"It doesn't sound like the end to me, Max. Wounds like that go deep."

"Yes, but it's been a long time. They're under a lot of scar tissue now."

"I'm sure," Gerd said, deciding not to push. Max only seemed to be comfortable making light of what must still be healing, even now. "When was the last time you saw Katherine Kowalski?"

"Hmm, I don't even know. Graduation, I guess."

"No lingering feelings for your first flame?"

"No. Just for the taste of cinnamon suckers."

"Have you ever told anyone that story before?"

Max thought about that for a minute. "No, I haven't," she finally said, as though it had just occurred to her. The waiter brought their falafel sandwiches and she spent a couple of minutes savoring the first bite. "I've alluded to it, but I've never told someone like I just told you."

"Were you ever friends again with any of those people you used to know?"

"My old clique?" Max chewed and thought. "I knew some of them in passing but I was never close to them again. Which was okay with me and was the point of my telling you this. They aren't really friends if they're more concerned about appearances than they are about you. You're better off without them."

"I agree, but this has just been such a big, sudden change, you know? It's not just that people have stopped talking to me. It's like I've become a total social outcast as fast as you can snap your fingers. I mean, my phone barely even rings anymore unless it's you or Cat or Leah or my family."

"Do you think anyone's just more shocked than anything else and they'll come around?"

"I doubt it. I don't even know that I'd want them to now, not if they're going to insult me to my face like that. You know?"

"Yeah, I do. I'm sorry, Gerd. I've been thinking about how you'd react to this, not how this might react on you. I know how much it stings to watch people turn the other way, and sit at home alone, wondering if you'll ever have any friends again." She took Gerd's hands. "You will, though. You'll have more and they'll accept you for who you really are. I'm very proud of you for making such big changes with so much courage."

"Thank you, Max. It's good to hear you say that." As she found herself growing entranced, looking into Max's eyes, Gerd considered telling her how important she'd become in her life in such a short time, how much she needed her, how much she wished Max would call more often just to say Hi, how was your day? But her intuition told her to keep those things to herself, to let Max need her too. Telling her how much she wanted her attention might make Max feel pressured. Gerd sensed an independent streak in her, that she would bolt at the first indication that someone *had to have her* in her life.

Breaking her gaze, Gerd drew her hands away, wiping her mouth with her napkin. Max went back to eating. If she sensed any of what Gerd was thinking, she didn't mention it.

"Ow!"

"What happened?"

"This isn't good."

Gerd hurried into the kitchen. Max was leaning over her trash can, holding one hand to her lower back. "Can you stand back up or does it hurt too much?" Gerd asked.

Max's face worked through a grimace as she raised up very slowly. "It'll be okay. Something caught for a minute. It happens sometimes. I just need to lie on the floor and let it relax."

"What if I rubbed it for you and then you lay on the floor?"

"You'd do that? I mean, you know how?"

"I certainly do. My mother has a bad back. I've been in the massage business for years. Besides, I owe you after what you did for my foot."

"As good as that sounds, Gerd, I don't think I'm going to be up for any pointers tonight. I'm in a little too much pain."

"I wasn't talking about pointers," Gerd told her, smiling. "I was just talking about giving you a massage."

"Well, okay then, I accept your offer. Work your wonders on me." Moving very gingerly, Max went into the living room. "Where do you want me?"

Gerd sat against the couch, spreading her legs out so that Max could back up against her. "Draw your knees up and your back won't be so tense. That's better." As she began to knead the knotted muscles, she felt something she hadn't noticed before. "Your back is crooked, isn't it?"

"A little bit. I have scoliosis."

"I knew a girl in school who had to wear a brace. Did you?"

"Yeah, I wore one for a few years. It was short. It looked like a hard plastic corset. You couldn't see it."

"That's why you move the way you do," Gerd realized.

"You mean how I'm rigid sometimes?"

"No, I mean how you make your movements look more graceful than most people's. There was a time when you couldn't bend. And," she ran her hands from Max's shoulders to her forearms, "that must be why you have such incredible arms."

"Well, what about these?" Max asked, putting her arms down by Gerd's legs. "These muscles are a sure combination of riding your horse and some kind of dance."

"I took ballet for ten years with Madame Porzikova."

"Now I know what accounts for that anaconda clench you put on me in the heat of the moment."

"Excuse me?"

"Perhaps you haven't noticed that you've cracked a few of my ribs. Ow!"

"So sorry. Did I gouge one of your cracked ribs?"

"I believe gouge is one word for it."

"I'll behave now. I promise." Max grew quiet as Gerd massaged her more deeply. Gerd could feel her muscles relaxing. "Max, are you still with me?" she asked after awhile.

"God, you're good at this. Remind me to throw my back out again sometime."

"It's getting late. Do you mind if I stay? I don't think I can summon up the energy to drive home."

"Yeah, just stay here," Max told her, leaning her head against Gerd's shoulder and sighing.

Max woke up with one of her arms asleep. Gerd was lying on it. Could she move it without waking her? Wait a minute, Max thought. There's no pain in my back. There's a woman lying in my bed, on one of my arms, unfortunately, who got me to relax so much that I actually feel better the same night. That had never happened before.

As she lay there, Max remembered something her friend Sadie had said. They'd been looking at the astrological chart Sadie had done for her. "When it comes to relationships, you need someone who wants to get involved in your creative endeavors, a details person, like a manager maybe."

"What if I don't want someone messing around with what I'm doing?"

"Max, you don't mind sharing what you're best at with other people. Don't you want to be with someone who does the same for you?" Sadie had asked.

Max looked down at the top of Gerd's head. What if she wants to get involved in the things I do? I can already tell she's more organized than I am. She'd probably make a great manager. Am I really ready to let her into my life that much?

I already want to see her more than I've ever wanted to see anyone else, Max thought. I've let her cook me dinner, help me with my laundry, give me a back rub. I even feel at ease around her, most of the time. Hell, look at the way we're sleeping all curled up. I've never held anyone this close before. I've never let anyone put my arm to sleep. What if she starts wanting more from me than what we already do?

I know how it'll start. She'll want to hear from me more. Then she'll want to move in together. I can just tell. Am I ready for that? I don't think so. I really like my space. I want to sleep late, play whatever music I'm in the mood for, sit up late reading in bed, walk around going over my lines out loud. I don't want someone around all the time. I don't want to be tied down. I don't want to account to someone for my whereabouts every time I go out. Maybe this is all moving a little too fast. Maybe I should get up and go for a drive.

Gerd opened her eyes. "Did you have a bad dream, treat? Your heart's pounding."

"Yeah, I did," Max said, sliding her arm out from under Gerd. "I'm afraid you cut off some of my circulation."

"Sorry. I guess I got too close. You're so comfortable. What was your dream about?"

"I can't remember. Don't worry about it. I'm turning over now so we don't have to amputate in the morning."

Gerd scooted close to Max's back, spooning her this time, as she slid her arm around her waist. Before she dropped off again, she noticed Max's heart was still beating fast.

Backstage, waiting for places to be called for the Sunday matinee performance of *Oh Coward*, Max and Raney stood in their long, sheer black dresses having a disagreement. Luckily–since they weren't far from the audience–the orchestra was playing louder than the disagreeing. Max had just found out that instead of waiting to go out with Gerd and her after the show, Raney and Constance had gone by Gerd's apartment the day before. "What possessed you to do that?"

"I was doing a survey for my women's studies class," Raney

said, avoiding looking at Max. Instead, she watched the stage left
wings where Roger and Byron stood in their tuxedos. Roger was
re-tying his bow tie for the umpteenth time.

"Why does your survey include a west Knoxville apartment com-
plex when there are thousands of women on campus?"

"You have to get a cross section for a survey to be worth
anything. It made perfectly good sense."

Behind them, Eve was helping Sara check off a list of props
stored in an old wardrobe trunk. "Hats with feathers?"

"Check."

"Champagne glasses?"

"Check."

"I cannot believe you did this," Max snapped at Raney. "I told
you we'd go out with you today."

"Well, we wanted to get a jump on things. So sue us."

"God, everybody just has to get in on the act, don't they?" As
Sara snapped the trunk shut, Max stubbed her toe on it. "Ow!
Jesus Christ."

"Sorry," Sara apologized.

"What do you mean, everybody has to get in on the act?"
Raney wanted to know.

"First I come into the green room and Eve starts telling Byron
how Gerd has caught me."

"I didn't say 'caught,' " Eve said.

Max ignored her, continuing to complain to Raney. "Then I find
out that you're investigating her behind my back. I wish everybody
would just get out of my space and leave me the hell alone. I can
judge who's worthy of my time myself."

"We're at places," Sara interrupted.

"Now?" Max demanded. "Can't we hold for five minutes?"

"We already did. We're at places."

"Oh, good. I can hardly wait to go on."

"Max, you've never even given me a chance to say that we
really like Gerd."

Max only responded with a long exhale. They stood waiting while the lights grew dim.

"This should be a fun show," Eve said.

After the performance, Gerd stood in the green room trying not to feel awkward. She was remembering the last time she had been there with Richard, and wondering if everyone around thought she was Max's new "conversion." She couldn't get what Susan, the costume shop manager, had told her out of her head. They'd gone to lunch with Max after one of her fittings. "Theatre people are big gossips in a small family, Gerd. I'm sure most of them will really like you but they'll pick you apart from head to toe first." Standing here now, Gerd kept thinking she felt eyes boring into her.

To make matters worse, she wasn't sure how to act around Max in public these days. Part of her wanted to be open, to hug Max and kiss her just as she would've done with any of her boyfriends. The other part of her knew that she wasn't ready to be that open about a gay relationship. In fact, most people here weren't that open about gay relationships. This was Knoxville, after all, not San Francisco. What did Constance and Raney do when they greeted each other? she wondered.

"It shouldn't be too much longer now," Constance said, coming up beside her.

Gerd smiled. "That's good."

Constance leaned close and whispered, "Dykes just take their make-up off. The straight girls have to put all theirs back on." As Gerd shook her head slowly, Constance grinned. "You do know I'm just kidding, right?"

"Of course I do."

"Here come our two favorite cast members now."

It had taken longer than usual for Max and Raney to get changed because they'd argued some more and then apologized to each other.

As Gerd watched them, trying not to be obvious, Raney and Constance clenched hands, looking each other in the eyes. Constance gave Raney a smile that communicated pride and desire, and Raney returned it with a very satisfied, almost private smile.

As soon as Gerd saw Max's face up close, she could tell something was bothering her. "You were terrific," she said anyway as she hugged her.

"Thanks. I'm glad you liked it," Max said, hugging her back without her usual warmth.

"You two were splendid," a woman from the audience said, walking up to Max and Raney from behind.

"Thank you," Raney told her.

"Gerd, I need a drink of water," Constance said. "Join me?"

Gerd followed her to the water fountain in the hallway. "It seems like they've disagreed about something," Constance said after taking a few swallows.

"I thought so too. I hope they get over it soon. I'm hungry." They both laughed. "Okay, I hope they get over it because I don't want to see such good friends mad at each other."

"Oh, they'll be fine," Constance assured her. "Actors are always starving after a show. The need to go out and eat has ministered to hundreds of bruised and swelled egos. What're you hungry for? I've got a yin for Chinese."

"Constance, that was a horrible pun."

"No, it was brilliant."

Max and Raney came out to the hallway. "We're starving," Raney told them, as they couldn't help smirking. "Let's figure out where we're going."

"I really like them, Max," Gerd said, when Raney and Constance pulled out of the parking lot. They'd dropped them by Max's car after stuffing themselves at a restaurant called the Great Wall. Raney had nicknamed it One Guy Cooking because one man made all the food on the spot when you ordered it. "Raney and Constance are both interesting and they make a neat couple."

With a slight moan, Max leaned against the driver's door. "I concur, as Constance would say."

"You're really wiped out, aren't you?"

"Yeah. The show took a lot out of me today."

"I'm very glad I came to see it."

"That's good."

"Are you glad I was there?"

"Of course I am. Why? Did you think I wasn't?"

"What's bothering you? I can tell something is."

"Well," Max paused for a moment, deciding not to mention the "Max is caught" conversation she'd overheard, "I found out about them dropping by to survey you right before the show started."

"And you didn't like that?" Gerd was careful to ask it like a question rather than something surprising.

"No, I didn't. People don't need to be poking around in my affairs without me knowing about it." Gerd looked stunned. Max hurried to apologize. "I'm sorry, Gerd. I'm so sorry. That didn't come out like I meant for it to."

"Okay," Gerd said in a very unsure tone.

"What I meant was, I feel very private about my romantic interests, and Constance and Raney know that. They've always respected that before, too. But this time, instead of waiting until I said we'd like to get together with them, waiting until we were comfortable doing that, you know?" Gerd nodded because Max seemed to be waiting for her agreement. "They went behind my back and inspected you. I don't appreciate them sneaking around, for one thing. And I also don't appreciate them treating you like a piece of meat that needed to be graded." Max looked away toward the tree-lined street that stretched alongside the theatre parking lot. It felt good to get that off her chest, but she wondered if Gerd thought she was overreacting. In fact, what if Gerd decided this whole situation was just too complicated for her? Max didn't want that to happen. She knew she didn't.

Gerd was trying to adjust to seeing this new side of Max. Also, she wanted Max to rethink things without Gerd saying, "That's not how it is." As Max stared at the trees, Gerd shifted from one foot to the other and let the tension ease for a minute. "Max, I really don't think they were treating me the way you think. Can I give you my perspective?"

"Yes."

"They were dying of curiosity," Gerd began, choosing her words carefully, "because I'm very different from the women you usually date. They wanted to see me in my own place without you around so they could get an idea of what I'm like. I know it may seem underhanded, but what I picked up on was how much they care about you and how concerned they are that this is a good situation for you. They didn't want to find out that you were seeing a rich, straight girl who was just enjoying rebelling against Mommy and Daddy for awhile. They wanted to know that their Max wasn't being strung along." Max was looking thoughtful, still leaning against the car door, but she wasn't saying anything. "Can you look at it that way?" Gerd asked, after giving her a moment.

"I think so," Max told her, finally looking back at her. "I really hadn't thought of it like that."

Relief flooded Gerd as she leaned against the car door too. "They caught me off guard, though, just showing up at my door like that. I didn't even know they knew where I lived, much less that they'd want to drop by for a visit."

"I guess I must've told Raney you live in Willow Dale."

"I guess you must've, yes."

"I don't remember, Gerd, honestly."

"Um-hmm," she teased, smiling up at her. "You know, once I got over the fact that they'd come by to check me out, I enjoyed their visit. I'm serious that I like them, Max. They're friendly and both of them are smart, plus they're funny together. They're so different. They do make an interesting pair. And they care about you so much, Max, which is something I can really appreciate."

"I see." Max reached over with one arm, drawing Gerd into a

hug. They stood like that, just wrapped around each other, for a moment.

"I'm wiped out too, treat. I'm heading home."

Looking into her eyes, Max brushed a lock of hair back from Gerd's face. "Gerd, don't let me scare you. I howl at the moon sometimes, but I'm worth waiting for the next morning."

"I'll bear that in mind."

Chapter Nine

As the season changed from spring to summer, Gerd learned about all sorts of useful things that were new to her–rainbow flags, upside-down pink triangles, the meaning of "family," the existence of "the community," and books, magazines, films, and meeting places she'd never even dreamed existed. She got to see Max and Raney play at more clubs, along with doing the summer run of *A Little Night Music*. She even discovered that she had perfectly good gaydar. She'd just been ignoring it for years.

At times she felt like Alice dropped into Wonderland, only the people in this world seemed sane and she didn't feel the need to get back to her former life. Well, not to get back to it completely, anyway.

She got to know some of Max's many friends better, too, particularly Raney and Constance. Almost everyone Max was close to was female, although many of them were straight. Gerd was glad there was a mix. Her transition would've been much more difficult, she thought, if all Max's friends had been gay.

Among the people she'd spent time with was Sara, who stage-managed a lot; Eve, who acted and wrote; Gail, who acted and sang; and Christine, who designed lighting. Then there was Sadie, an astrologer and Reiki practitioner; Andrea, a massage therapist, and Aggie, a handwriting analyst, who both worked for the pro-choice coalition; Lana, an artist studying technical editing; and Gina, a writer who worked at one of Max's favorite bookstores.

Max's phone rang often when Gerd was over, and Gerd became accustomed to the call waiting beeping when she called Max. What seemed like late-night hours to Gerd was prime chatting time to Max, a true nocturnal if Gerd ever knew one. In fact, most people had learned that was the best time to catch Max at home. When

Gerd would inspect Max's calendar, covered with upcoming outings, she'd wonder if her own life was downright dull. But Max didn't seem bored. She certainly made time for Gerd and there was no indication that Gerd's more laid-back social life slowed Max down.

One day, as Gerd listened to Max talking her way out of one of two separate outings on the same night, she realized that she couldn't remember the last time she'd gotten into a similar situation. In fact, as she thought about it, she still just didn't get that many phone calls. Cat and Leah remained the only members of her former circle that she heard from regularly. Mostly she did school and Max and Max's social life. Every so often when she was solo she got together with one or both of her old stand-bys for dinner.

God, how did this happen? she thought. I'm completely im-mersed in Max. I'm enjoying myself, but what if things don't work out for some reason? My new life is built on a one-brick foundation. I'm not so sure I've come out. I think I've just fallen in. Well, that could be remedied, she decided. Her first step was to invite Max over for dinner with Cat and Leah.

Three weeks and two cancellations later, they finally gathered around Gerd's table for salad and casserole.

"Gerd, this is wonderful," Leah said through a mouthful.

Cat looked across the table, her eyes filled with amusement. "You said it, sister."

"Thank you," Gerd laughed. Trying to be discreet, she nudged Max's shin under the table. "What about yours, treat? Do you like it?"

"Uh-hmm," Max answered quickly, like a kid whose mom reminds her to say thank you.

"I was beginning to think this dinner was never going to happen," Cat said. "Were you really busy those other times, Max, or did you just want Gerd all to yourself?"

"No, I was really busy," Max blurted, turning a bit red as Gerd let out a sound of protest and turned a bit redder.

"Catherine," Leah cautioned, "we've hardly met the woman and you're already embarrassing her."

"Max, I only tease people I really like," Cat assured her.

"That's good to know." Max's spoon slipped through her fingers and bounced off the rim of her bowl. She smacked her hand across it to keep it from falling on the floor. All the dishes jumped. "Sorry," she said to the surprised faces looking at her. "I'm sorry I had to cancel those other times. I didn't know we were going to have rehearsal or get that gig."

"I've really enjoyed the two gigs we've been to," Leah told her. "I like saying the word gig. It makes me feel cool." Cat and Gerd chuckled at her.

As she watched a slice of tomato miss Max's mouth and fall back in her bowl, Gerd had to suppress another chuckle. She'd never imagined Max would be this nervous over a simple dinner with her friends. "Do you know if you're playing at Tomato Head that Saturday night?"

"No, I haven't heard back from Raney yet. I should know something by tomorrow."

"I just remembered," Leah said, "I wanted to ask you about the origin of your last name. Ivers isn't very common."

"Well, the Ivers themselves were very common," Max said abruptly. Cat spat her wine out as she laughed. Leah got tears in her eyes trying not to choke. "The name is English but we don't know who came over here first. It seems that pig farmers were more concerned about mixing their slop than keeping records of relatives."

"Makes sense to me," Leah said.

"Do you want some more wine, honey?" Gerd asked Max.

"Yes, darling," Cat cut in. "I've spat half of mine into my napkin."

Max smirked. "I'd like some too, please." Shaking her head at them, Gerd re-filled their glasses. As Max picked hers up, it slid through her fingers, toppling onto the table with a bounce. Everyone scrambled to mop the wine up before the seeping red puddle could make too many stains. "Shit. I mean, oops. I'm sorry, Gerd."

"It's okay. We'd better do something about your shirt, though."

Max looked down at the wine staining her shirtfront and one sleeve. It was one of her favorite shirts, a white linen and ramie blend that she'd picked out one day with Gerd.

"Let's soak it in the bathroom and see what we can find in my closet," Gerd said, heading toward the hallway.

"Excuse me," Max said to Cat and Leah.

In the bathroom, Gerd stood filling the sink. "God, I've turned into Charlie Chaplin out there," Max said, pulling the door shut and leaning against it.

"Honey, why are you so nervous?" Gerd cut the water off and turned around.

Max started unbuttoning her shirt. "Because these are your best friends. I want to impress them."

"Sweetheart, they're already impressed with you. You don't need to make a bigger splash of yourself."

"That was awful. You've been hanging around Constance too much."

"You're just jealous because you didn't think of it."

"Absolutely."

"Honestly, Max, I'm serious that Cat and Leah like you. Why would you think that you have to try so hard for them?"

"They're from your . . . your circle. I mean they're . . ."

"Blue-blood, horse-riding, sorority sisters," Gerd suggested when Max seemed at a rare loss for words.

"Yeah, and I'm a small-town dyke with no pedigree who changes her own oil. Aren't they afraid I just want you for your money or something? I don't mean they're shallow . . . but they look out for you like Constance and Raney do for me, right?"

A smile crept across Gerd's face. She shook her head. "When I first met you, and they didn't even know you, they warned me to be careful because I was dealing with someone new. But just in the few times they've seen you play they've really liked you and they've seen how happy we are. Plus, they can tell you're no gold digger."

"They can? How?"

"You passed Cat's test. You paid for your drinks, and mine, too. Cat says if someone wants to clean out a blue blood the first thing they do is let her pay for all the drinks, like drinks don't cost anything."

"But my drinks were on the house. I only really paid for yours."

"Well, I know, but that's a minor technicality according to Cat."

"I see. Does Leah have a test too?"

"Yeah, but I'm not supposed to tell you about it."

"Well, now I have to know."

"Okay, okay. Her test is called the butt test. She got it from her grandmother."

"The butt test?"

"Yeah, whenever Leah starts seeing someone her grandmother always asks her if he has enough tail to hold up his britches. Translation, does he have a good butt? Leah's taken to using the same criteria for other, um, involvements as well."

"And I pass this test?" Max asked, putting her arms around Gerd as she looked into her eyes.

A strong wave of desire swept through Gerd. She considered telling Max to get her well-filled jeans off, but Cat and Leah were right down the hall. God, those green eyes were emitting strong currents. Sliding her hands into Max's back pockets, she pressed her close. "Treat, you bring it to a whole new scale."

Max was leaning down, with her lips so close Gerd felt her breath.

"Gosh, this casserole sure is getting cold out here!" Leah called.

"Maybe they can warm it in the bathroom!" Cat added.

Gerd and Max both started laughing. "Let's finish dinner and save each other for later," Max said.

"You're on."

*   *   *

"Gerd?"

"Max?" Gerd asked into the phone. "You just left."

"No, Gerd, it's Gerald."

"It's too early for whatever you want, Gerald. I'll call you back later."

"No, Gerd, don't hang up. I called to warn you."

"Warn me about what?"

"Mom and Dad are on their way down there right now to talk some sense into you."

"Why? Oh shit, did they hear you last night?" Gerald had called and woken her up last night but Max hadn't stirred so she'd stayed on the phone awhile. During part of the conversation they'd been talking about her being a lesbian.

"No, it was Mom, and then she told Dad."

"Shit, Gerald. I thought I could at least trust you to be careful."

"I was. I was down in the basement and they'd gone to bed. I didn't think there was any way anyone was going to hear me."

"So how'd it happen then?"

"When Mom opened the door to come down the stairs she heard me saying something like 'my sister, the lesbian.' She snuck in on me, Gerd, I swear. I never heard her. She didn't even turn on the lights. I hung up and all of a sudden the lights came on and there she stood."

"Shit, shit, shit. How much did they get out of you?"

"They know you're gay."

"What about Max? You didn't tell them about her too, did you?"

"I had to. Mom heard too much. I couldn't cover it up."

"Goddamnit, Gerald. I don't fucking believe you."

"I stuck up for you, Gerd. I told them how happy you are. And I told them how much I liked Max, too."

"Oh yeah, I'm sure that's why they're on their way down here right now, isn't it? Because they're just dying to congratulate me."

"Gerd, I tried every way I could think of to get them to listen to me. It just didn't work. Mom kept saying they're going down there to put a stop to this right now. I'm sorry."

"I've got to go, Gerald. I've got to figure out what to do."

"Do you want me to come down there?"

"No, just stay put. You've done enough already."

"Gerd, I really am sorry."

"I'm sorry too. I know you didn't mean for this to happen. Just don't say anything else to them, okay? And don't call me from the house again if they're there. I'll talk to you later."

Gerd sat in sweatpants and a T-shirt, waiting for her parents to arrive. She'd called Max to tell her what was happening. Should she have taken her up on her offers, she wondered? The first had been that Max would kidnap Gerd for the day, in case she wasn't ready to deal with her parents' resistance and possible strong-arm tactics. No, she told Max. Might as well do it now. Maybe it was a sign that she was ready to. The second offer was that Max would come over so she didn't have to face her parents alone. But Gerd had felt that this was her stand to take. Even though Max was an important part of her life, she needed to show them that being a lesbian was her own identity, not someone else's influence. Gerd inhaled deeply as she put her head against the couch. Could she do this? she wondered. Was she really ready?

A few minutes later she heard their voices outside as they walked across the breezeway and knocked on her door. She inhaled deeply again, getting up to answer after telling herself that they would've seen her car. There was no way she could pretend she wasn't home.

"Why, there's our girl," her father said when she opened the door.

Her mother was kind of smiling and frowning at the same time. Gerd knew the frowning was because she wasn't really dressed. Well, not what her mother would consider dressed, anyway. "My goodness, sweetheart, you look like you just got out of bed."

"I haven't been up too long, I guess." Of course, and this is what always got her about her parents: they may have left home in a hurry, but they both looked completely put together. Her father was in his usual sports shirt and slacks and her mother had on a pants suit with a matching bag.

As they hugged her, she wondered if they were as uncomfortable going through the motions as she was. "I bet you're surprised to see us here," her mother said as they sat on the loveseat.

"No, I'm not, actually," Gerd told her, even though her heart was pounding. She'd promised herself to tell the truth, no pretending. She sat on the couch. "Gerald called and told me what happened." Their smiles disappeared. Her father looked startled and unsure what to think. Her mother looked angry. It was what Gerd had expected.

"Well, after what he was saying last night we had to come," her mother began. "Gerd, we're just real concerned about you now. You've fallen in with the wrong sort of people . . ."

"What sort of people are those?" Gerd interrupted.

"Lesbians," her mother said, as her eyes narrowed. Gerd had never heard the word said in her presence with such venom. "They've got you all turned around."

"I'm not turned around, Mother."

"Oh yes, you are. We knew something didn't add up when you gave Richard that ring back. Now we're beginning to put two and two together."

"I didn't give Richard's ring back because I met some lesbians. I did it because I realized that I'm a lesbian."

"Gertrude Mercer Mackenzie, how can you sit there and say a thing like that to your father and me?"

Her mother was struggling with disbelief, Gerd knew, but it was anger that was showing on her face and coming through in her voice. Anger that her daughter was defying her, that she would dare say this or think this or be this. And that she wouldn't listen to reason now made it even worse. "It's about time I told you I'm gay. It's the truth and I've been hiding it and hiding from it for years."

"It most certainly is not the truth. It's a sick lifestyle is what it is and no daughter of ours is going to take any part in it."

"It's not a lifestyle. It's part of my identity. I was born this way. I denied it for years because I knew you wouldn't approve, but I finally just couldn't deny it anymore."

"You know it's wrong to live this way, honey," Gerd's father spoke up, but his tone was much more compassionate than her mother's was. "It says so right in the Bible. Now why would you want to do a thing like this?"

"It's this girl you've met, isn't it?" her mother demanded. "She's put you up to this."

"Max didn't put me up to anything. She just asked me if I thought I might be gay."

"See there, we were right." Her mother glanced at her father before looking back to Gerd. "She put this idea in your head."

"No, she didn't put anything in my head," Gerd said, noticing her voice was rising. "It was already there. That's the whole point."

"Honey, we just don't believe that, now." Her father squeezed his knee as he always did when he didn't want his concern to show.

"Well, I wish you would believe it, because it's the truth. Max is a wonderful person and if you met her you'd like her."

"Your brother has already sung us this tune," her mother snapped impatiently.

"Then maybe you should listen to us," Gerd snapped back.

"Why? You're not listening to us, now are you?"

Reason with her more and snap at her less, Gerd thought. "I listened to you for over twenty years, but you have to realize that I'm an adult now. I'm not always going to do everything you tell me to."

"If you think you're going to live this way with us supporting you, you're wrong," her mother told her. Her voice had gone from argumentative to cold and blunt.

Gerd was scared by the tone and by the implications. "What does that mean? Are you cutting me off?"

Her mother drew herself up, looking Gerd right in the eyes. "Either you quit this gay business or we're not paying your rent and your bills and your school anymore."

"I can't believe you'd try to blackmail me like this," Gerd blurted.

"Now listen, it's not blackmail, honey," her father said. "We're just trying to tell you we're serious. We don't want to do this now." He looked at her mother as though to assert his authority. "Surely you can see you've just made a mistake."

"All I can see is that you're being bullies. Do what we say or we'll take away the things you need."

"As *I* said," her mother said, emphasizing the "I" to reassert *her* authority, "we intend to nip this idea of yours in the bud right now. And if it takes withholding your money from you to make you see the light, then we will."

Gerd was so crushed that she felt unable to do anything but speak. And that was enough of a struggle. "Keep your money, then. It doesn't make me who I am anyway. Not having it won't make me straight."

"I hope you realize just what a mess you're making of your life, young lady," her mother snapped as she stood up.

"I hope you realize just what an awful thing that is to say to me," Gerd managed to answer.

"C'mon, Cam, let's go. We'll just let her think about this for awhile and see if she doesn't change her mind real fast."

Gerd's father stood, looking as if he wanted to say something else to her. But when her mother opened the door and looked back at him, he shook his head and walked out.

*   *   *

Gerd sat on the floor, not moving, for she didn't know how long after they'd gone. She knew she was in shock. Fragments of their conversation flitted through her head but she found she was unable to think about it. She just heard it like a tape being played repeatedly. Finally, she dialed Max's number with her numb fingers.

"Hello?"

"They're gone. Can you come get me?"

"I'll be right there."

Max was scared as she drove Gerd back to her place. She was afraid that Gerd was going to break down any minute, and Max had always been afraid of getting close to fragile people. But Gerd didn't break down. Her eyes just leaked some tears as she gave a brief version of what had happened, finishing with not knowing how or when her parents meant to check up on her again. Still, Max could sense that she was on the verge of falling apart. She reached over, put her hand on Gerd's and squeezed. Gerd squeezed back, falling silent the rest of the way.

When they got inside, Gerd sat in one of the kitchen chairs before Max could even tell her to come into the living room. What do I do? Max wondered, as Gerd sat staring into space. What the hell do I do for her now? "Do you want something to drink?" No response. She looked at the cabinet anyway.

"Could I have some water?" Gerd asked suddenly.

"Sure." The task of getting the glass and some ice gave Max relief. At least it was an action. It was something she could do for her. She took it to Gerd, who seemed to forget to reach out for it. Now what? "I'm just going to put this on the table and go to the bathroom for a second, okay? I'll be right back."

It was when she was about to flush the toilet that she heard the glass shatter on the floor. A horrifying wail followed. Max ran into the kitchen. Gerd sat there, holding her face in her hands, rocking back and forth while she cried in great, racking sobs. Max carried her into the den. Sinking onto the couch, she cradled Gerd against her, rocking her gently without saying a word.

Gerd's crying went on until Max began to worry that she wouldn't have a drop of moisture left in her body. The muscles in her back were knotted to the touch. Eventually, Max began to rub her fingers in light circles over the tension as she hummed.

Gerd grew quieter. The thought "How long have I been at this?" suddenly formed in her head. Her breathing was labored. Then she noticed her ear was against Max's heartbeat. It was so nice and steady. It was the most comforting sound she'd heard all day. And I'm so warm, she thought. This is how it must feel in the womb, cradled and warm with a heartbeat right up close. She pressed her forehead to Max's chest. Then she noticed Max's shirt, soaked through with tears and lovely snot from her runny nose. Maybe that combination is a lot like the inside of the placenta, Gerd thought, nearly laughing. "I've ruined your shirt." She looked up.

"No, you haven't. It'll wash." Max freed one arm, took her shirttail and dried Gerd's tear-soaked face. Then she raised her chin. "No matter what anyone has said to you today, you are a beautiful person and you're loved and accepted in this house for being exactly who you are."

"Thank you, Max. That means more than you know."

"You have so much to offer, Gerd. So many good things."

"My parents seem to have forgotten that."

"It won't last, I bet. They're angry right now and they're focused on that. Give them time."

"Max, I don't have time," Gerd said with desperation in her voice. "They're cutting me off, remember? Even if I work full time there's no way I can afford to pay my rent and bills and school all by myself. Maybe I can move in with Cat. I don't know. I don't know what I'm going to do." She looked down, getting scared all over again.

Max was scared too, of what had popped into her head. Do I dare? she thought. I want to help her. I know that. Maybe I could share my space with her. I could at least try, I guess. She put her hands on the sides of Gerd's face, making her look into her eyes. "What if you moved in here?"

"Are you sure?" Gerd asked, finding it hard to believe that Max was willing to commit to something so serious. "I mean, I'm a wreck. My parents will be at me. I need help moving. I don't have an income right now. I . . . ."

"I'm sure I want to help you," Max cut in. "Even with all those things going on. And letting you move in here is the best way I can think of to help. So, what do you say?"

Tears welled in Gerd's eyes again. "I say yes. I love you, Max. This isn't how I meant to tell you, but I really really love you."

"I love you too," Max told her, kissing her tears and wrapping her arms around her more tightly. Questions spun inside her head. What if this doesn't work out? What if I'm not ready? Do I really love her? Do I really want to live with her? Then Gerd burrowed into her and Max decided to put those questions aside for now so she could concentrate on helping.

Chapter Ten

Gerd sat outside her apartment office, waiting for the manager. The sign on the door said she was "showing an apartment, back in five minutes." It had been more like twenty.

Feeling shaky, Gerd wished for a cup of coffee. How am I going to explain why I need out of my lease? she wondered. I've been cut off. I can barely bring myself to form that sentence in my head. No way is it going to come out of my mouth. Maybe I should just go. I'm not ready for this.

As she stood up to leave, Sharon, the manager, walked up with a beaming couple in tow. "Come on in," she told Gerd. "Have a seat. I think we'll be done in just a few minutes."

Feeling compelled now, Gerd sat on the couch, listening to the Beamers start the nitty gritty details of filling out an application and putting down a deposit. Where should I get boxes? she worried. Oh that's right, Max said Gina could get some. How many will I need? How will I afford a truck? What if . . .

"What can I do for you, Gerd?" Sharon asked. Looking up, Gerd realized the Beamers had left without her even noticing. "You know, you look awfully tired. Would you like some coffee?"

"Yes, please. That would be great."

Gerd met Sharon at the coffee maker, gratefully adding cream and sugar and wrapping her hands around a nice, warm mug. She took a big sip. "Can we . . . can we go in your office?"

"Sure." Sharon shut the door behind her and sat at her desk. "What's wrong, Gerd? You look like something's bothering you."

"I . . . um. I need to break my lease, Sharon."

"What's happened? Are you changing schools?"

For a moment, Gerd toyed with the idea of telling her yes. It would make everything so much easier. Yes, that's it, I'm transferring. I just found out I'm accepted. I've got to move now so I can start classes this fall. Wouldn't you know they'd wait till the last minute to tell me? She looked back up at Sharon's expectant face. No, there was no reason to start lying now to someone she barely knew when she'd told the truth to her own parents. "No, I'm staying at UT. It's just, my parents and I, we've had. . . ." She set her mug on the desk, took a deep breath, and made herself look at Sharon again. "We've had a big misunderstanding. They're not going to support me anymore." Tears came to her eyes. She blotted them with her shirtsleeve.

Sharon handed Gerd a tissue from one of her desk drawers. "Oh my gosh, what happened? I'm sorry, Gerd. I don't mean to be nosy. That's just such a shock."

"You can say that again." Gerd wiped her eyes and blew her nose. "They found out something they don't like." Looking across the counter, she wondered how much to tell Sharon. She was hoping to get sympathy. In fact, she needed to get sympathy because there'd be fees she couldn't afford. But what if Sharon were just disgusted or offended? Well, that was her right, wasn't it? Hadn't that been Max's point that night her supposed friends were so insulting at the Falafel Hut? Anyway, she needed to get the process of moving started, no matter what Sharon thought of her or wanted to charge her. "What happened is that my parents found out I'm gay and they're very shocked and upset with me. They don't want to support me now and I can't support myself at the moment."

Sharon definitely looked shocked. She cleared her throat, looking Gerd up and down as if her appearance had changed from a minute ago. "So, you're looking for something cheaper?" she finally asked.

"I have to. I'm not sure when I'll find a job." Sharon just kept looking at her. Gerd felt she'd been sized up and found lacking. "So what do I need to do to break my lease? I've got to move as soon as possible."

"Well, you really can't give notice till the first of the month and then we charge the next month's rent as a termination fee."

"So, you're talking over a thousand dollars." Gerd drank more coffee. How on earth am I going to work all this out? she wondered. "Can I make payments on it? There's really no other way I could give it to you."

"When are you planning on moving?"

"By this weekend. I just need to get some boxes and start packing."

"Did all this just happen with your parents?"

"Uh-huh, yesterday."

"So if I called them, they could confirm this story?"

Story? Gerd wanted to burst out. This is no story! This is my fucking life. She sat clenching and unclenching her hands, trying to calm down. "I'd rather you didn't call them, but yes, they could confirm what I've said."

For a moment, Sharon didn't say anything. She was looking away, frowning, then she was looking at Gerd, frowning. Abruptly, she pushed her chair back from her desk. "Let's go look at your apartment, Gerd."

On the way up the hill, Gerd realized that Sharon must've heard a lot of rent scams. She had to cover her bases. It didn't really make Gerd feel better, but at least she understood.

After a quick inspection of the apartment, Sharon cleared her throat, facing Gerd with her hand on her hip. "Okay, here's what I'll do. If you'll be moved out by next week I'll forfeit next month's rent and your termination fee. I think I can rent this place again pretty quickly. It's in good shape. But you'll have to clean everything up real good and forfeit your deposits."

So much for being able to start out with a little money, Gerd thought. Oh well, at least she wouldn't be in debt. "Okay, it's a deal."

Sharon fiddled with the cord on her arm that held her office keys. "I, uh . . . well, I've got to get back down there. Let me know when you've got everything out. There'll be some paperwork for you to sign."

"Okay." Gerd let her out, closing the door quickly behind her.

From a business standpoint, she knew Sharon had made a good decision. But the fact that she couldn't meet Gerd's eyes as she left or wish her well made a stronger impression on her than good business.

"Wait a minute, wait a minute," Max's older sister, Abbie, was saying as they came to the bottom of a hill on the paved green way at Lakeshore Hospital. Abbie had come into town for a morning meeting and then met Max for lunch. "Remind me, how long have you known this girl?"

"Since February," Max told her, trying not to sound as defensive as she felt. "And would you stop calling her a girl? She's twenty-one years old."

"That's a girl to me, Max. Anyway, are you involved with her?"

"For crying out loud, Abbie, she's moving in with me," Max said, waving her arms and almost hitting a passing jogger. Then Max noticed Abbie's eyebrows were pinched together just like their mother's were sometimes. Was it because she was interrogating Max or because the water treatment plant beside the green way smelled especially bad this afternoon? "Do you really think we wouldn't be involved?"

"What I think is that this has gotten awfully serious in an awfully big hurry, Max. That's what I think."

"Well, that's just how it happened. I didn't plan for her parents to cut her off so she'd need a place to stay, you know?"

Abbie avoided a pile of dog poop as they rounded a curve. "It doesn't sound like she needs a place to stay. It sounds like she needs a place to live."

"Fine, pick my words apart. The point is, she has one."

"Does she have a job?"

"She's going to look for one."

"Has she gone through the classifieds?"

"Look, Abbie," Max snapped, slowing down because she was annoyed, "all this just happened this weekend, okay, and it's only

Monday. She's breaking the lease on her apartment today and then we're picking up some boxes so she can start packing. She'll look for a job as soon as she can. Now give it a rest, would you?"

"Max, I worry about you," Abbie told her, keeping up with her more easily now. "I'm always going to worry about you. I'm your big sister. It's encoded in my genes. That's what the second X is for."

I will not laugh, Max thought. "I know you worry. You just drive me crazy sometimes."

"You drive me crazy a lot of the time," Abbie assured her. "I think that's in the little sister gene pool. Must drive big sister crazy at every opportunity." Looking over, she saw a grin on Max's face.

"I must be doing a good job then, huh?"

"Amen." Abbie gave Max a playful shove. "Let me tell you what I'm concerned about, okay? This is important."

"Shoot."

"This gir . . . sorry, woman, has just come out recently. You're her first girlfriend. Her parents found out before she was ready to tell them. And she's having to make major changes in every part of her life as a result."

Why did Abbie always have to look at the down side of everything? "I know it sounds like a lot when you put it that way . . ."

"It is a lot, Max," Abbie cut in. "That's what worries me. I'm afraid it's going to backfire on you. And I don't want to see that happen."

Max was quiet for a moment as she considered her sister's concerns. She understood them. Abbie wasn't crazy. So how did she explain how she felt about this new direction in her life? "Abbie, I'm not saying I know what's going to happen, but you'd just have to know Gerd. She's the kind of person you can believe in."

"I hope you're right. I know how much you like her. I've known that just from talking to you on the phone."

"Really?"

"Sure. I want to ask you something else. Is she in love with you?"

"She says she loves me and I believe her."

They started up another hill. "What about you, Max? Do you love her?"

"I don't know," Max admitted. "How does love feel?"

"Well, how do you feel?"

"Excited. Scared. Both. Hell, I don't know." Max tried to breathe easier as she leaned into her stride. This last hill was so steep, but she loved the way she felt invigorated afterwards. "See, Abbie, the thing is, I think I want things to work out, but I've never done this before. What if she moves in and then I realize I don't want to share my space? What if she decides she really is straight after all? What if her parents come down here and cause a big scene?"

"A Max scene?"

"Abbie, I'm being serious here."

"I know you are. I've just never seen you have such a case of the hots for someone."

"The hots? You sound like Mom."

"You're going to sound like Mom too someday, little sister. It's only a matter of time."

"Know-it-all," Max said. "Do you think I'm doing the right thing?"

"I don't know, Max. If you ever trick me into coming up this hill again, I may kill you."

"Want a hand, weakling?"

"I'm not that desperate yet." Max grinned at her. "Like you said, things have been going so quickly it's hard to tell. You have a big heart, though, and I'm proud of you for doing so much to help someone else. And I think you have it in you to make a relationship work for the long haul. Just keep your eyes open. And look both ways before you cross the street."

"And make sure you wear clean underwear," they said together, able to laugh now that they'd reached the top and made it back to the parking lot.

"I've got to get back to Nashville, kiddo. Kurt will be waiting on me and I've still got reports to write before I get some shuteye."

Max walked her over to the Nissan Pathfinder she'd coveted from the first time she'd even heard about it. "Be careful, Ab. Thanks for lunch . . . and the advice."

Abbie gave her a quick hug and climbed behind the steering wheel. "Call me late some night and let me know how things are going."

"I will," Max said. As she watched Abbie pull out, she wondered how things would be going when she made that call. She wished she knew already.

At Max's two days later, Gerd was trying to concentrate on the positive things she had going for her, like an interview the next day thanks to Cat. "You're sure this looks okay?" she asked Max and Cat, modeling her Anne Klein suit in the living room.

"Yes, it looks fine." Max turned back to looking through packages of guitar strings.

"Is that all? Just fine?"

"Terrific. Fantastic. Stunning," Max added quickly without looking again.

"You're a sight to behold," Cat threw in.

"Great, I'll be overdressed."

"Gertrude, that's a perfect suit for your interview, you look gorgeous in it, and you know all that. If you don't get a little more confident, I'll be forced to strangle you," Max told her.

"I'll already be dressed for the funeral," Gerd joked half-heartedly. Max was right. She would do fine in the interview with Cat helping her cram. And she knew the suit was a good choice. But she felt so unsure about her entire life right now that she just needed overwhelming support and attention. Didn't Max get that?

Max caught her arm and pulled her close. "After two questions, they'll hire you." She gave her a quick kiss. Gerd felt so much better that she snatched another one.

"Sorry," Cat mumbled as she was caught staring.

"You're just jealous," Gerd teased her, grabbing a pillow off the couch and bopping her on the head.

"Not over you. Puh-lease." Cat jerked the pillow out of Gerd's hand and bopped her back.

"Okay, okay, truce. Are you going to help me prep for this interview or not?"

"Yes, if you're through with your fashion show."

Max picked up her guitar. "I'm going to practice on the porch."

"Didn't you break a string?"

"No, those new ones are for Raney. Mine's got all six, see?"

Over the next two hours, to the strains of Nanci Griffith, Rickie Lee Jones, and original music, Cat filled Gerd in on all the details of the office where she worked. Called Dunwoody & Associates Financial Services, it was a partnership of four men who served as financial advisers and overseers of investments as well. Cat was a part-time assistant to Butch Dunwoody's assistant, and now one of the other advisers, Cal Tompkins, needed a second assistant too.

Cat told Gerd everything she could possibly need to know about the way things were done, what she'd be responsible for, and every nitty gritty detail about Cal Tompkins. Then she made Gerd repeat everything back to her, filling in and making corrections as needed. Finally, she quizzed her on stocks, bonds, money markets, mutual funds, T-bills, secured loans, amortization rates, and exchange rates, to name just a few things. Gerd called it quits after two glasses of tea, half a legal pad of notes, and a headache that was pounding with the force of a sledgehammer. Still, she managed to voice her profuse thanks before retreating to the bathroom for extra-strength Tylenol.

"How'd she do?" Max asked, as Cat came out onto the porch.

"Great. There're still things she wants to go over, and she's nervous as hell, but she knows what she's talking about. I think she's going to get this job."

"Thanks for all you've done to help, Cat. You're a very good friend."

"It's easy to help someone when you love her, isn't it?"

Max looked down for a moment. When she looked back up she had a shy grin on her face, as if she'd been caught doing something she really enjoyed. "Yeah, it is."

"See you later," Cat said, stifling a laugh as she headed for her car. "Oh hey, this weekend we're moving her stuff, right?"

"Yeah, be at her place bright and early Saturday morning."

"You got it."

"I thought you were asleep already," Max said when she came into the bedroom to find Gerd's eyes wide open with the light still on.

"I need to be, but it just isn't happening."

"Why not?" Max brushed her hair.

"Probably because I'm lying here worrying about things."

"Things like what?"

"I'm wondering if my parents will ever speak to me again or have anything to do with me."

As she pulled the loose hair from her brush, Max looked over at Gerd. "Do you really think they won't? I know I haven't met them, but I have a hard time believing that."

"Okay, doctor, what I really think is that they'll speak to me again and I won't want to hear what they have to say."

"That's understandable. What else is bothering you?" Max looked at her face in the mirror.

"I'm afraid moving will be a mess because I've never moved my stuff without my parents' help before."

"And what did I tell you about that?"

"Not to worry because your friends from the theatre are going to help."

"Gerd, they're your friends too, and I promise you, theatre people are probably better than anybody at moving stuff. They're efficient, they're careful, and they're used to working from start to finish."

"What if I haven't packed enough?"

"G, you've been over there packing for two days straight and Gina said she's got more boxes saved if we need them."

Gerd sat up. "Max, I'm scared to death about this interview too."

Turning from the mirror, Max went to the bed and put her arms around Gerd. "Let me ask you something. Is there anything you haven't done to get ready?"

Gerd was quiet for a moment. "Not that I can think of."

"So what're you worrying about?"

"Well, I keep thinking about what'll happen tomorrow. You know, how many things could go wrong."

"I've done the same thing before, Gerd, many times. But let me ask you something. Why do you keep thinking about how things could go wrong? Do you want them to?"

"No, but . . ."

"Then why spend your time thinking that way? You did your work getting ready. Now, let it go."

"I want to, but . . ."

"But what?"

"I'm so worried about money, Max," Gerd said, looking up at her. "I mean, I need an income now, tomorrow, you know?"

"Why?" Max asked, brushing a lock of hair away from her eyes. "Why do you need an income tomorrow?"

"Because I don't want to live off you. And I don't want my parents to be right when they said I wouldn't be able to make it without their money."

"So by earning money, you'll be able to show everyone what you're capable of. Is that it?"

"Yes."

"Gerd, anyone who wants to can already see what you're capable of."

"How's that? How do you see it?"

"I see it because you're here. You're in this bed because you kissed me, broke off your engagement, started seeing me and came out to your friends and family, all in less than six months. I have a crystal clear picture of what you're capable of. And if you want an income to support yourself then I know you can have that too, because you're doing what it takes to achieve it."

"Wow. You know something?"

"What?"

"I'm a pretty amazing person."

"Yes, you are," Max agreed, kissing her forehead.

"And you're pretty amazing too."

"Why's that?"

"Because you realize just how amazing I am."

Max started laughing. "I've created a monster."

"A monster who loves you," Gerd assured her, pulling her down for a kiss.

"I love you too. Now, you need to get some sleep." Max slipped her clothes off, climbed into bed and turned out the light.

Gerd snuggled into her arms, trying to relax. Several minutes later she finally said, "Max, how do you get your brain to turn off when you're worrying?"

"I think of something I'd rather do instead."

"Like what?"

"Like this." Max slid her arms around Gerd, slipping her fingers inside her so gently that Gerd let out a pleasant sigh. Drawing their legs up close, Max rocked Gerd with long, gentle strokes until she came, drifting afterwards into a very calm sleep.

Max sat at the box-office computer, deleting old entries from the address file. Susan, the costume shop manager, sat behind her repairing a couple of stock costume pieces.

"Sounds like you gave Gerd a pretty good pep talk to me," Susan said, after Max related their conversation from the night before.

"I think so too. I kind of startled myself. I didn't know I had all that in me."

"I suspect there's a lot more where that came from," Susan told her, grinning when Max shot her a look of surprise. "Hey, did you hear, Eve and Derek left Sara's together last night?"

"Derek? I thought she was going out with some guy at the library."

"She is."

Max turned to see Susan raising her eyebrows as she bit off her strand of thread. "So, were they just leaving at the same time or were they leaving together?"

"Together, it looks like."

"Don't you two have anything better to do than gossip?" Max jumped, not knowing anyone was at the window.

"C'mon Gerd, you know us," she heard Susan saying as Gerd, who was positively beaming, leaned on the counter.

"So how was . . ." Max started to ask.

"I got the job!" Gerd burst out. "I got the job. I got the job. I got the job. I start Monday."

"Yes!" Max yelled, jumping over the counter. She threw her arms around Gerd, whirling her in circles. "I'm so proud of you!"

"Max, did I just step on your foot? Where are your shoes?"

"I don't care, Gerd. I don't care. This is cause for celebration."

"We could go out to dinner tonight."

"Not tonight. Now."

"But you're working now."

"She's not that indispensable," Susan said as she stepped out of the office with her costumes. "Go home with the woman. And congratulations." She started toward the costume shop.

"Thank you," Gerd called to her. "It's good to see you. Let's do lunch again soon. I really enjoyed it last time."

"So did I," Susan called back. "We'll do that."

Meanwhile, Max had hopped back over the counter, saved the file, turned off the computer, turned on the answering machine, locked the sliding glass windows, found her shoes, and locked the door.

"Are you sure this is okay?"

"I think they'd prefer that we celebrate at home instead of in the office."

"I see."

"Race you."

"No, treat, let's get there together."

"Next box," Gerd called out of habit. They'd been moving her things all day.

"That was the last box," Gail told her.

"You're kidding." Gerd sprawled on the floor with a sigh.

"Max," Gail called.

"Yes," came Max's voice from somewhere in the apartment. Gerd couldn't tell where exactly.

"The good news is, we've got your girlfriend moved in. The bad news is, I think we killed her in the process."

"Can she be revived?"

"I'll check." Gail leaned over, looking at Gerd upside down. "What if I made coffee?"

"Um," Gerd considered, "no, I need more."

"Gail, you ninny," Eve called out as she beaned her in the head with a wad of newspaper, "we just finished moving. We need beer and pizza."

"Beer and pizza!" Raney and Christine and Sara and Byron and Hal chimed in.

"I concur," Constance agreed after everyone had quieted down.

Gerd sat up, looking at them with a smile. "I was wondering why so many people stayed after we got done with the heavy stuff."

What really amazed her was how quickly and smoothly everything had gone. Max had been right. Theatre people were terrific movers. All of them were good at packing, and Christine, who handled lighting instruments for the shows, was an expert when it came to anything fragile. She also did a beautiful job coiling up all the cords. Gail and Eve and Raney labeled and carried countless boxes, waiting for Gerd's directions on how to handle and place everything. Sara and Byron had lent their trucks. Along with Hal and Max, they'd moved all the furniture she could keep. Goodwill had picked up the pieces she was willing to part with the day before. Max's apartment wasn't big enough for all her furniture and Gerd's too.

Cat and Leah had helped Gerd figure out where to put things once the boxes got to Max's, although they'd both left in the afternoon. Cat had a date to play tennis with a guy she was jokingly calling her ball boy. ("He's young and he has very good . . . hands," she'd said.) Leah was going to help her younger sister, an incoming freshman, move into her dorm room. Constance, who'd spent the morning finishing a summer project at the Art and Architecture building, had come over to help Gerd make the final decisions about where her things should go.

Sometimes it had been a tight squeeze, but the place looked wonderful, Gerd thought, surveying as far as she could see without getting up. Constance had a great eye for placement. It was possible that Max wouldn't recognize the place anymore, but she'd get used to it. They both would.

"Did I hear something about beer and pizza?" Max dropped on the floor beside her.

"Yeah, the natives are restless." Gerd whispered in Max's ear, "Can we afford this? I mean, I want to, but there are a lot of people to feed."

"Don't worry, G. I have some money stashed from our last gig."

"But Max, I don't want you to tap into that on my account."

"Gerd, it's on the account of all these people who helped us all day. But there's a problem."

"What's that?"

Max looked around the living room, then cupped her hands to her mouth. "Has anyone seen my phone?"

Chapter Eleven

A few days later, they were trying to get used to sharing each other's space, but Gerd thought it was going well. The amount of cover on the bed had been some cause for concern. Gerd liked a blanket or comforter all the time. Max got too hot for anything more than a sheet blanket. After one night of trying a blanket and waking to discover it neatly folded so it covered only her, Gerd suggested two sheet blankets. This seemed to be working better. Max kept Gerd very warm. Constance insisted that in time they wouldn't snuggle up together every night, but Gerd was content to enjoy it for now.

Max had told her the first day they'd ever spent together that she really didn't talk much in the morning. In fact, Max didn't even like to get up early. Gerd had learned to get up and do her own things, and not to worry that Max was mad. Likewise, Max had learned that Gerd "wilted," as she called it, by about midnight. So she was studying at night and working on her music during the day.

Max had done several things for Gerd. She'd changed her oil, fixed the door that had jammed on her boom box, and repaired a lamp with a short in the switch. In return, Gerd had tried to come up with favors to do for Max. She'd put a few of Max's pictures in some extra frames she found. When she'd showed Max, who hadn't noticed, Max grinned, putting her arm around her. This spurred Gerd on.

One evening when she got home from work, she rearranged all Max's music alphabetically–tapes, CDs, everything–before Max came back from a poetry reading. Deciding this was a vast improvement, she also rearranged everything in the old wardrobe where Max kept her guitar supplies, sheet music, and some sound equipment. "What do you think?" she'd asked, the minute after Max came home.

"Where's the song I was just working on?" Max wanted to know, thumbing through the sheet music.

"Well, I put it all alphabetically, see, so it's under 'U' for Untitled."

"But Gerd, there are five other Untitleds here."

"I know. Now they're all together."

"Yeah, but I want the one I'm working on to be on top. That way I know which one's the latest."

A feeling as if a teacher had called her down came over Gerd as she watched Max slide the latest Untitled out and put it back on top. "I'm sorry, treat. Have I messed everything up?"

"No, I'm just going to put a few things back, okay?"

"Okay."

But later, as they got ready for bed, Max gathered Gerd into her arms like always and Gerd fell asleep thinking that everything was going to be fine.

Max woke up later with the feeling that something wasn't right. She lay there for a second, growing slowly more conscious and eventually noticing that her arm was asleep. Once again, Gerd was curled across it. How was it that something so uncomfortable was becoming one of her lover's favorite things to do?

As she slid her arm free, Max decided she might as well go to the bathroom. But on the way through the living room, she stubbed her toe against the coffee table. That's got to move, she thought crossly. Trying again, she made it into the bathroom only to hit the same toe on the magazine stand that was now by the toilet. Why did Gerd have to put a magazine stand right there?

With her toe throbbing, Max went into the kitchen for some ice. As she stood with her foot over the sink, Max looked at the dirty dishes. She didn't recognize a lot of them. Of course they were Gerd's, but it suddenly began to feel very odd to her that her own sink was filled with someone else's dishes. When am I going to get used to this, she wondered, mugs with sunflowers, a casserole dish? I've never made a casserole in my life.

After dumping her ice, she hobbled into the living room. The first thing that caught her eye was her music cabinet. It annoyed her to think that all the things in there had been moved. Trying to find something else to look at, her eyes could only see things that were new, different, rearranged, or moved. There were her CDs and tapes in this whole new order. There were her pictures in those gold frames across the mantel. That isn't the way I had the pictures set up, Max thought. Those aren't even my frames holding my pictures.

Feeling the need to leave, Max tried some calming techniques instead. Closing her eyes, she breathed deeply and thought the word "relax" over and over until she felt more peaceful. Maybe I just need to get some rest. I'll get into bed and get some more sleep. I'll feel much better when I wake up again.

But as she went back into the bedroom, Max realized it wasn't going to work. There was Gerd taking up half the bed. She was out there. She was in here. She was everywhere. Max grabbed a pair of jeans and a shirt from her closet. I've got to get some space of my own, she thought. A night drive had better do the trick.

A couple hours later when Max pulled back into her parking space, she saw Gerd sitting against the porch railing. There was a worried, angry expression on her face as she raised her head. Max turned off her headlights, wondering how best to handle the situation, as Gerd got to her feet. Let her know she doesn't need to worry about me, Max thought. Let her know I don't want to be worried about. Let her know I have to be able to come and go when I please.

Climbing out of her Jeep, Max headed for the porch. "Hey G, what're you doing out here?"

"Worrying out of my mind," Gerd snapped. "Where have you been?"

"I just went for a drive."

"In the middle of the night?"

"Yes."

"Why didn't you tell me you were going?"

"You were asleep."

"You couldn't leave me a note?"

"I didn't think about it. I'm sorry. You look cold. Let's go in."

"Now you're concerned about me?"

"Of course I'm concerned about you."

Gerd turned to go in. "God, what a night."

"Okay, so are you upset because I left or because you didn't know where I was?" Max asked, closing the door behind them.

"Both."

"Look, I didn't think you'd even wake up before I got back."

"Well, I did."

"I also didn't think you'd be mad about me being gone."

"I'm not mad, damnit. I'm worried. Don't you think you'd be worried if you woke up and found me gone in the middle of the night?"

"I guess," Max said. She'd never thought about anything like that.

"I mean, I didn't know whether to call someone now or wait till morning or go looking for you or what."

"Wait a minute, wait a minute. Why would you do any of that? Did you think I wasn't coming back?"

"I didn't know what to think, Max."

"For God's sake, Gerd, you could see I didn't pack a suitcase," Max argued. "I just went for a drive."

"But I didn't know where or what for and it's the middle of the night!"

"I needed to think, okay?"

"Why couldn't you think in the living room?"

"Because I needed to get away for awhile."

"Get away from what? Me?"

"No."

"Well, what then?"

"This," Max said, gesturing in a wide sweep. "All this."

"What're you talking about?"

"This isn't my place anymore. You know what I mean? Your dishes are here. Your magazine stand is here. Your picture frames are here. You're here. My place is full of . . . you."

"I don't understand. You asked me to move in."

"I know that."

"Have you changed your mind?"

"No, no, it's not that."

"Well, what then? It sounds like you don't want me in your space."

"Listen, Gerd. It's like this. I woke up tonight and you were on my arm again. I went to the bathroom and nearly broke my toe on your stuff. I went to the kitchen and there was more of your stuff. It doesn't even look anything like my stuff." Max put her hand to her face and rubbed her eyes absently. "I never had anyone here to stay before, you know? This has always been my place. I kind of panicked. That's why I went for the drive, to get some space of my own."

Gerd's eyes filled with tears. "I was afraid of this. Everything's moving too fast and now I'm in your way." She stopped and took a deep breath, feeling a tear start down her cheek. "I'll move out as soon as I can find another place." Turning quickly, she started away.

Max caught her before she could take more than a step. She didn't even think about it. She was more concerned about Gerd's feelings than her own; she had to tell her. Turning Gerd back, Max wrapped her arms around her.

"Honey," Max said, "I don't want you to go. While I was out I realized that I'd never come back from a night drive to having someone at home before."

"But you said you flipped out because I'm here."

"I know and I did. But when I thought of you in bed and how you always snuggle up to me, I missed you. I wanted to come home and crawl in bed with you. And find a way to keep my arm from going to sleep. Together."

"Are you sure, Max?"

"Yes."

"I mean, are you sure you want to be together?"

"Yes, Gerd, I am."

"Because if you're not sure I'd rather know now."

"Gertrude," Max said, tilting Gerd's face up till she was looking her in the eyes. "I'm sure, even if I am still getting used to you being in my life. I'm sorry I made you worry. I didn't mean to and I should've known you would. Please forgive me. I was pretty naive thinking this would feel like our place right after you moved in. It's been my place for two years. It's going to take some time to adjust. I promise, I'll talk to you next time I start to worry."

"I hope you do," Gerd blurted, "because the other night when I couldn't sleep you helped me." She sniffed hard to keep her nose from running. "It just hurts to know that when you couldn't sleep you left without even telling me."

"I'll bear that in mind next time. But I'm still going to need to take a drive every once in awhile. It's just the way I'm wired, G. Sometimes I need solitude somewhere else. I used to go driving even when you didn't live here."

"You did?"

"Yes, and that doesn't mean I'm not coming back. I swear I'll leave you a note next time. Please don't move out."

"Okay, I'll go back to bed," Gerd said as she kissed her. "How about that?"

"Sounds good to me."

"Are you coming?"

"I'm right behind you," Max told her, laughing at herself for trying to make Gerd laugh, which worked. Which made her laugh.

* * *

Gerd kicked her shoes off the minute she got in her car. Her feet hurt and her legs hurt and her back hurt and her head hurt. Plus, she had cramps. Otherwise, she'd had a great first full day at work. She'd helped prepare an investment proposal today and had done so well that Mr. Tompkins had discussed the client with her at length, but she just wasn't used to working all day yet. Her classes all fell on Tuesdays and Thursdays, so she was scheduled to work full days Monday, Wednesday, and Friday. Thinking about that, Gerd exhaled tiredly. This was the last weekend before classes started for fall semester. She was looking forward to lying around doing nothing.

As she turned onto their street, she noticed a familiar car parked behind Max's Jeep. Was that Gerald's Acura? The sunlight shone into her eyes as she pulled in to park. That was his car, all right. What was he doing here? She fished her shoes out and got her purse off the passenger seat.

"I'm saying he's a better passer than Bradshaw," she heard when she'd opened the door.

"And I'm saying you're full of it. Bradshaw could do everything Montana can and he's got Super Bowl rings on his fingers too."

"I'm home," Gerd yelled, pushing the door shut. "What's my little brother doing here?" Instead of more debating she heard two people scrambling to their feet.

Max came through the doorway first. "Hi there. How was your day?"

"Long," she said as Max hugged her. Gerald stood in the background, looking sheepish. "Where do Mom and Dad think you are?" she asked him.

"At Tony's."

"I see. Does Tony know this?"

"Sure he does."

"Did you remember to call and say you made it okay?"

"Yeah, I did."

"How long have you been here?"

"I don't know." Gerald looked at Max as though to say, please rescue me from my big sister.

"Maybe for about an hour," Max told her. "He called from the road and I told him how to get here."

"What if Max hadn't been home?" Gerd wanted to know.

"What does that matter? She was."

"I still don't get it, Gerald. What made you pull a stunt like this?"

"God, you sound like Mom."

"Oh, I do not."

"Yes, you do. You sound just like her."

"I do not sound anything like my mother!" Gerd exploded. "Now what are you doing in my apartment?"

"I wanted to apologize, okay?" Gerald told her. "I feel really bad for giving you away and I thought if I came down maybe I could make it up to you somehow."

"Well, so far you're not doing a very good job. And all this yelling is making my headache ten times worse." He started to say something but she interrupted him. "And don't tell me that I don't have to yell."

"Do you want some aspirin?" he asked quickly.

"Do you have any aspirin?"

"No, but I'll go get you some." The puppy dog "I've been kicked too many times but I still want to please you" look on his face was just too funny. Gerd started to laugh. The more she laughed the funnier his face got. "What'd I do?" he wanted to know. He was laughing too.

"You don't need to get me any aspirin, G. We have some in the medicine cabinet."

"Well, what do you want me to do then?"

"Come over here and give your poor sister a hug." He put his arms around her. "I'm glad to see you, G." He gave her a tug that lifted her to her toes. She twisted one of his ears. "But I don't appreciate having to cover your ass to Mom and Dad, especially right now."

"Ow! I'm sorry. I didn't think of that."

"How sorry are you?"

"Ow! Very sorry."

"Sorry enough to spring for a pizza for dinner?"

"Yes, now let go."

"With extra cheese and breadsticks?"

"Yes, yes. I'll tickle you, Gerd, so help me god."

She grinned as she let go. "Sucker."

Glancing over the top of her paperback, a bodice ripper she'd bought for brain candy, Gerd saw a scene that amused her. Not far away, Max and Gerald were taking a breather from throwing a football. To her credit, as Gerd thought of it, Max had been making Gerald do most of the running. He was bent over with his hands on his knees, in fact. But if you followed his gaze, he was also watching a woman in short shorts walking alone up the hill toward them. Max gave him a thwack on the arm. He thwacked her back.

"Go long, you slack-off."

"Are you sure you can get it that far?"

"Better get moving or you won't catch up." Gerald started running, slowly. As she laughed, Max blew a kiss back to Gerd.

The football arched toward Gerald in a beautiful spiral. What an arm Max had, Gerd thought. As Gerald sped up, he crashed right into the short-shorts woman. She landed on her butt with him on top of her. They looked like an un-posed Rodin sculpture. Laughter broke from Gerd's lips as Max, grinning widely, dropped beside her on the blanket. "You did that on purpose, Maxine."

"Yes, I did. He had looked so much I thought he might as well touch."

"You know, it means a lot to me that you and Gerald get along so well."

"It means a lot to me too. He's a good guy. He really cares about you."

"And that woman he doesn't even know," Gerd commented, as she watched him walking away from them with Short Shorts.

"Boys will be boys."

"I suppose so."

The rest of the weekend seemed to go quickly. Max, of course, had phone calls to return when they got home. Still, they made it to a late movie. Gerald sat down front, as much to give them time to themselves, Gerd suspected, as to get what he insisted was the best possible view of Michelle Pfeiffer. The next day they went to brunch at the Copper Cellar, then watched the first half of the Redskins playing the Giants. Gerd insisted that Gerald needed to start for home after that. She was paranoid that he'd get there late, something Tony's parents wouldn't let happen.

As Gerald got ready to put his bag in the car, Gerd quizzed him about his packing. "Do you have your toothbrush?"

"Yes."

"Are you sure?"

He held it up. "Yes, I'm sure."

"Put it back in there then. Do you have all your clothes?"

"Yeah, I got the stuff you washed plus the rest."

"What about your . . ."

"Gerd, I have everything, okay? I have everything."

"I'm just making sure. If you leave anything, God knows when I'll get it back to you."

"I guess so."

"How're Mom and Dad doing?" Gerd asked. It was the question she'd been both wanting and dreading to ask all weekend.

"They're okay. Kind of upset still, I guess. Dad wanted to call after you left that message about moving in here and getting your job but Mom said she wasn't ready to talk to you yet. I don't know why he can't just call you himself."

"What did they think of what I've done?"

"I think they were kind of surprised. Mom's been so sure you'd be calling to tell them you were wrong and needed help. Dad seemed kind of proud about the job. I think that's why he wanted to call you."

"I'd like to talk to them, you know? I mean, they can be hard to take sometimes but . . . I still love them."

"They love you too, you know." She nodded. "Maybe you'll hear from them sooner than you think." He put his bag in the trunk and got something else out. "Here, I've got something for you. I almost forgot."

He handed her a small jewelry box. "I hope you haven't spent money you don't have," Gerd said.

"Just open it and quit worrying."

Inside was a charm, a rainbow flag with gold edges. "Oh, for my bracelet. Gerald, it's beautiful. But you didn't have to get me anything."

"I just wanted to, okay?"

"How did you know about the flag?"

"I asked this guy at school and he ordered it for me. I think I have to go out with him now." Gerd was still laughing as Max walked up. "I have something for you too," Gerald said. He pulled a video from behind his back.

The Greatest Moments of Terry Bradshaw," Max read off the cover. "Cool. This'll be perfect for Sunday nights by the fire." Gerd rolled her eyes. "After you're gone to bed," Max added, nudging her. "Thanks, G."

"You're welcome."

"You'd better get on the road, young man."

"You're right."

"Give me a hug," Gerd told him. How did her little brother get so grown up? she wondered, as she kissed his cheek and felt the stubble of his beard. "Be very careful. Don't speed, especially in Virginia."

"I won't. I grew up there too, remember?" Gerald reached out to high five Max. "Take care, Max. Thanks for everything."

As she returned the high five, Max grabbed him in a headlock.

"Remember who took you in when you ran away from home, bud."

"I will."

"Be good, Gerald."

He got in the car, returning their waves as he turned toward the interstate. Gerd twined her arms around Max's neck, feeling herself rewarded with a clinch from behind. "Are we still going to Constance and Raney's party tonight?"

"I guess we should. But we have all afternoon to uh . . . get ready. Get each other ready?"

"Umm, that's the kind of talk I like to hear."

Max stood in Constance and Raney's backyard talking to Gail and Sara while she drank a beer. "Max!" someone yelled.

"Cat?" Max peered into the dark. "Hey, I thought you couldn't make it."

"Where's Gerd?"

"She's inside."

"Can I talk to you for a minute? Privately?" Max frowned, but she nodded. "I'm sorry to interrupt," Cat said to the others, who were looking at her with very puzzled expressions.

"Is everything okay?" Gail asked.

"No. You'd better come inside," Cat told her, hurrying to catch up to Max. "I'll be there in a second."

Inside, Gerd had retreated to the bathroom to dab alcohol on a handful of mosquito bites. She couldn't believe that everyone else could be outside talking without getting bitten while she was being devoured. Constance had a theory that mosquitoes went for women on the rag because they had more blood. Could it be true? Gerd wondered, chuckling as she tossed the cotton ball in the trash.

Walking into the living room, she joined a conversation with Raney and Eve. "Do you remember that skit Allie wrote for Max and me for All Nite Theatre?" Raney was saying.

Eve nodded. "It's too bad you missed it, Gerd. Raney and Max were long-lost, identical-twin-sister nuns. It was hysterical."

"Yeah," Raney said, grinning, "I loved it. Allie says she might be recycling part of it for this screenplay she's working on."

"I hope she does. Do you think she'll come back here when she's done with grad school?"

"I don't know, but I want her to. I miss her."

"Last time Max talked to her, she said she wasn't sure what she'd do next," Gerd told them. Then she saw Max come through the door with Cat behind her. "I thought you had a date with your ball boy, Catherine." Why'd Cat look so upset? The strongest sensation came over her that something was wrong.

"Honey," Max began, slipping her arm around Gerd's shoulders, "Cat's got some bad news. Something's happened."

Max almost never called her honey. She and Cat both looked like they were in shock. Something was very wrong. Gerd's heart pounded so hard she could've sworn that Hal and Byron could hear it across the room. "What is it?"

Cat took her hand. "Your parents just called me because they couldn't get you. Gerald was in a wreck on the interstate." A whimper leaked from Gerd's lips as Max held her tighter. "A drunk man hit him from behind and he hit another car. He's in critical condition in the hospital."

"Oh my God," Gerd managed to say, although her throat felt as if it had swelled completely shut. Tears ran from her eyes. "When did it happen?"

"I'm not sure exactly," Cat said. "Sometime earlier this evening."

"Where was he?"

"I think your mom said he'd just come through Charlottesville."

"God, he was almost home. Why was that drunk on the road? What if he doesn't make it? Oh my God, we have to go up there, Max. We have to go up there. Now."

"We're going, honey." Max kissed her forehead, putting both arms around her as she cried harder.

Chapter Twelve

As they walked down the hallway toward the ICU waiting room, Max's legs felt too heavy to lift. They were still half-asleep from the way she'd turned sideways so she could hold Gerd while Cat drove and Leah rode shotgun. Raney had followed in her car so that Cat and Leah would have a way home. They were all waiting in the lobby to hear about Gerald's condition before they left.

In the car, Max hadn't noticed her legs' falling asleep. Her focus had been entirely on doing whatever would comfort Gerd the most. At times it was wiping her tears, at times it was letting her cry, and for long stretches Max had listened to reminiscences about Gerald or tried to reassure Gerd as she worried out loud.

But now that she was about to meet Gerd's parents for the first time, Max was getting preoccupied. What would they think of her? They knew she was coming, because Gerd had said so on the phone, but she hadn't heard any kind of response. Would they speak to her in a distant way, ignore her, yell at her to get out and leave them alone? She hadn't been looking forward to meeting them under good circumstances. Now, she was even more concerned.

Suddenly, Max remembered that it was Gerald she really needed to think about. He was the one fighting for his life after someone's stupidity had left him pinned in a collision. He'd come to visit them, without his parents knowing, just because he wanted to apologize in person. He'd given her a Terry Bradshaw video this very afternoon. Well, maybe it was yesterday by now. Damn, her eyes were getting a little teary. Max hated to lose her composure. She said a quick prayer for Gerald as they came to the waiting-room door, then gave Gerd's shoulders a squeeze. Gerd reached up, squeezing her hands back for a split second. Then they went in.

Everyone looked at them immediately. Max had never felt more uncomfortable. Making entrances onstage in front of packed houses didn't bother her. But this did–seeing the desperation in the eyes of these strangers she couldn't help. Gerd went straight toward a group that was huddled together across the room. "Mama," she said with a breaking voice.

A woman stood. Once her hair had been the color of Gerd's, Max guessed. Now it was lighter, most likely colored to hide the gray. Her face could almost be the mold for Gerd's, except for her pinched jaw line. Was the tension just because of Gerald, Max wondered, or was it always there? Gerd's mother stood there taking in her daughter, giving Max such a cursory glance that she almost missed it. Then she held out her arms to Gerd and everything about her seemed to soften.

Gerd and her mother stood there crying quietly, letting their tears soak each other's blouses. A man with snow-white hair and deep blue eyes that were recreated in Gerd's face put his arms around both of them. There they are, Max thought, the family unit. Now what do I do?

No one else in the group of people with them said anything. They glanced kindly at Max, then glanced away again. The worry and weariness were etched onto their faces so clearly they almost seemed to be wearing masks. There were as many empty coffee cups stacked on the table beside them as Max had ever seen in the theatre green room.

After a while, Gerd and her parents sat down, wiping their faces with tissues. Max sat too, glad to give her tingling legs a rest.

Later, after coming back from the lobby where she'd bought their drivers snacks for the road, Max found Gerd's family still discussing Gerald's condition. He was in a coma in intensive care. Immediate family members could see him only for a few minutes. "He's bandaged up so," Gerd's mother was telling her. "You can hardly even make him out in all of that. And . . . he's on a respirator. That thing's so loud."

"It's just real loud," Gerd's father agreed.

Max tried to keep listening, but as they discussed injuries, emergency medical procedures, and which doctor did what in minute detail, her attention wandered. She had nothing to add to the conversation. She'd been to hospitals before. She even had a good idea of just how serious Gerald's condition was. But they knew all that too. They just needed to say it out loud, to go back over everything as much for their own benefit as Gerd's. Plus, at some point during her mental side trips, Max realized that she'd never been introduced to anyone. Should she butt in? Should she go get coffee? Should she just take a walk? She honestly didn't know.

Gerd's mother looked at her watch. "It's almost time to see him again," she announced. "You go down there this time, Gerd. Your father can go with you."

Hearing that, even though she knew that only family was supposed to visit, Max felt invisible. Before she'd been uncomfortable, feeling almost naked under their gazes. But this was even worse. Summoning energy into her still-tired legs, she stood, not sure of where she was going, just that she had to get out of that room.

". . . Max."

"What?"

"I said I'm sorry," Gerd repeated. "I just realized I never introduced you to anyone."

"That's okay. You've been a little busy."

"Everyone, this is my roommate, Max. She brought me up here. This is my mother, Ruth, and my father, Campbell, and their pastor, Dr. Ivey, and these are our godparents, Frank and Sue Conlan."

"Hi. I'm glad to meet all of you. I just wish it was under better circumstances," Max said. Small talk had never been one of her strengths.

"Listen, why don't you girls go down there and see him together?" Campbell said.

"It's only supposed to be immediate family, Cam," Ruth blurted, although she was careful to keep her tone polite.

"I know that," he told her. "But I've been down to see him every time and hasn't nothing changed or the doctor would've told us. These girls probably need to stretch their legs. Besides, it might cheer Gerald up to hear some young people checking in on him."

"Well, maybe Maxine doesn't want to see someone with tubes and bandages all over him," Ruth replied in a sterner but still polite tone.

Max was hesitating when she heard Gerd jump in. "Mama, I'd like for Max to come with me. If you're sure that's okay, Daddy?" He nodded. "She cares about Gerald too. She came all this way and sat here while we ignored her."

"Well, whatever you think, dear," Ruth answered. She looked at Gerd first, then shifted to Max. Her eyes narrowed. That was the only way she was willing to tell her that she didn't want her going in to see her son. She wouldn't say anything in front of these people, wouldn't raise her voice or cause a scene. But she would make it perfectly clear to Max how she felt.

Max considered bowing to her wishes. Her son had been critically injured that night. Maybe she should respect Ruth's feelings. But then Gerd put her hand on her arm. "It would mean a lot to me, Max."

"Okay," she said, watching Gerd's expression, relief mixed with worry.

That first night, at the sight of her little brother struggling between life and death, Gerd grabbed Max's arm so hard she left bruises. Max said nothing as her fingers dug in. She was stunned too. Gerd tried to hold back her tears, but her tissue was soon soaked. In a few minutes, when they had to leave due to the time restrictions, Max held Gerd tightly until she pulled herself back together. Ruth turned out to be right about one thing. The respirator seemed incredibly loud.

*   *   *

Three days later they'd grown a little more accustomed to seeing Gerald pale and still and gauze-covered. He was hooked up to so many machines, Max was amazed that a single human body did the work of what looked like a whole factory.

It was hard being at the hospital. There was very little to do, the furniture grew uncomfortable, even if it didn't start out that way, and seeing Gerald still in the coma was unsettling at best.

Being at Gerd's parents' house wasn't much better, as infrequent as it was. It was more of a mansion than a house, as far as Max was concerned: six bedrooms, four bathrooms, a huge bonus room and an equally huge kitchen. But Max felt stifled anyway. The furnishings were so upscale she felt as if she'd stepped into a Showcase Home from *Southern Living*. Almost every room was filled with things Max wasn't willing to sit on, touch, or even breathe near. The china cupboard in the main dining room was every bit as intimidating as the deer's head in Campbell's study. The backyard, several acres of beautifully landscaped grounds as well as a pool, felt more comfortable to Max. Weeping willows, towering pines, and magnolias surrounded the yard's boundaries, providing plenty of shade.

Campbell was so preoccupied with Gerald's condition that he barely spoke. Max could sense that he was impressed by how she stayed with Gerd. But this was no time to try to form a bond with him. The only time Ruth quit worrying about Gerald was at home when she saw Gerd and Max together. She still never said anything impolite to Max, but her eyes shot deadly looks. What Max didn't know was if Gerd saw her mother's looks. If she did she hadn't mentioned it, and with her so concerned about her brother, Max didn't want to bring it up. It seemed too selfish.

To make matters worse, Max had begun to wonder if there were any point to her staying in Richmond much longer. She felt that she should. If your girlfriend's brother was critically injured, didn't you stay with her? Gerd needed her, she thought, and hopefully

Gerald did too. But Gerd had withdrawn into herself, and although Max didn't blame her, she didn't know how to help, either. With no change in Gerald, Max couldn't tell that she was helping him either.

Fall classes had started, along with rehearsals for a production of *The Crucible.* Plus, this month's bills would be due in a few days. Gerd had withdrawn from classes and taken a leave of absence from work. Maybe one leave was all they could afford.

What would Sadie say about this, Max wondered, that she didn't feel she was helping people if she couldn't see immediate results? Was this in her astrological chart somewhere, clearly mapped out if only she paid attention? Probably, she decided, leaving her doubts unspoken.

After breakfast on morning number four, Gerd and her father went upstairs, leaving Max and Ruth alone in the kitchen. "Would you hand me that salt shaker, Maxine?" Ruth asked, getting a canister from one of the cabinets.

As she brought the shaker to be refilled, Max made up her mind to say something. Being called Maxine since they got there was driving her crazy. "I really go by Max, Mrs. Mackenzie."

Ruth snatched the shaker. "Well, whatever you want, then. I don't know why a girl would want to go by a boy's name."

"It's not a boy's name to me. It's just my name."

"I see," said Ruth, but her tone said she didn't see because the very notion of a girl named Max was crazy.

Max plowed on anyway. "I really appreciate you letting me stay here. But I know it's uncomfortable for you. I just wanted you to know, if you want me to stay somewhere else I will. I mean, this is your house and I'll respect your wishes. But I plan to stay up here."

"Whatever for, dear? What can you possibly do?"

"Be here for Gerd and Gerald."

"Gerd doesn't need you here, in my humble opinion. Maybe if you would leave she would get over this crazy gay notion of hers.

Maybe Gerald would even come out of his coma if we could just concentrate on him instead of having to worry about her too."

"Your worrying about Gerd is your choice. I'm not causing you to," Max said quietly.

"Spoken like someone who's not a mother, my dear," Ruth replied in a chilly tone.

And for once, Max felt herself backing down to someone else's low opinion of her. "Fine, I'll get a motel room." She left the room, feeling smaller than she'd felt in a long time, diminished by those narrowed eyes.

All that day at the hospital, Max could tell Gerd was mad at her. It seemed to have something to do with reserving the room, but the few times they could've discussed it, Gerd went to get coffee or food instead. Finally, Max said that she was going to the motel. Gerd surprised her, telling her parents that she was going to follow Max over there, so she'd know where it was.

At the Budget Motel desk, check-in felt as if it took forever. They didn't spell her name right, couldn't find the keys, couldn't get the credit card scanner to work. Max wished Gerd hadn't come with her. She seemed dangerously close to losing her temper. Max heard her kick something on her way to the water fountain.

After an uncomfortably silent ride up in the elevator, Max unlocked her room. "Let me see what the phone number is."

"So is Mama right? Was it your idea to stay here?"

"Yeah, it was."

"Why?" Gerd demanded, as angry as Max had ever heard her.

Which was better, to answer the question or just run out the door and not come back? Max wondered. "Look, Gerd, it seemed like the best thing to do. I was uncomfortable in the house and they don't really want me there."

"Well, of course, Max. What did you expect?"

"This, I expected this, I guess. But that doesn't mean I could deal with it anymore. It's a wonder your mother hasn't bored holes through me with those looks of hers."

"You should've talked to me about this first."

"I was trying to do something for you, to make things easier on you." And me, she thought.

"You still should've talked to me first."

"Okay, I get it. I should've talked to you first. I guess I just don't have the hang of being a couple yet."

"No, you don't. What you've done is just what's best for you. What about me? I was having a hard enough time dividing my attention between home, where I'm waiting for my mother to unleash on me instead of just making little comments . . .' "

"What little comments?" Max interrupted.

"Oh, things like, 'I don't know why you'd want to share your room with her when we've got two perfectly good guest rooms she could stay in.' "

"Why didn't you tell me about that?"

"Because I'm worn out just from dealing with it. I don't even want to get into this right now. It's another whole discussion." Gerd stopped for a second to catch her breath. "Like I was saying, I've been having a hard enough time dividing my attention between home and the hospital, where I'm waiting on a miracle, I'm afraid. And now you're in a motel room. I don't have the energy for this, Max. I can't wait for you to come to your senses too."

"I never asked you to concentrate on me right now," Max said through the growing numbness she felt.

"Not in words, maybe, but in your actions you do."

There didn't seem to be any emotion on Gerd's face. It scared Max. "So, what are you driving at? Do you want me to go home?"

Gerd turned away. "I don't know."

"Gerd, the only reason I've been staying up here is for you and Gerald. But you make it sound like I'm just in your way."

"No," Gerd glanced back at her, "that's not what I said."

"Well, that's how it feels," Max insisted. "Look, I don't want to fight both you and your mother to stay up here. We should be thinking about Gerald anyway."

"I'm trying to," Gerd said, sounding tired and defensive at the same time.

"So am I, but . . ." What more was there to say? Wasn't the next thing to do very obvious? Why avoid it, saying it or doing it, Max thought. "Look, I'm going back to Knoxville for awhile."

"Maybe that's best." Gerd sighed as she shook her head. "I don't know anymore." She left without another word, just a sad, quick glance, before she pulled the door shut.

That, along with worry over Gerald and anger at Gerd's mother, was why Max finally fell, crying, onto the bed. But when she woke the next morning, with tears dried on her face, there were no messages.

Chapter Thirteen

Max was sitting on the brick wall behind the theatre. Her butt hurt and she knew the bricks were dirty, but she couldn't bring herself to move. There was no show tonight. It was Sunday. There wasn't even anyone in the theatre, as far as she knew, which was odd. Usually there were rehearsals.

She wasn't sure quite why she'd come here to brood except that she was tired of brooding at home alone or brooding in class where she forgot to take notes, wondering why she was even there. Plenty of her friends had tried to help by inviting her out or to their places to vent her frustration. But she pulled away from everyone instead, quit answering the phone, quit going to the door. Eventually she got what she wanted–solitude.

It had been two weeks since she'd come back. She'd only talked to Gerd once and all they'd talked about was how there was no change in Gerald. She'd thought about her a lot, rehearsed conversations, even picked up the phone several times, but she didn't dial the number.

It seemed that things had come down to a choice for Gerd: her family or Max. She'd gone with her family. Max realized that she couldn't blame Gerd or judge her or think she was weak for choosing her family. After all, look at their situation.

But at night, lying alone in bed just when she'd gotten used to Gerd being there, she couldn't help feeling hurt. Well, more than hurt. She felt catapulted right back into her Katherine Kowalski days, crushed, devastated, and unable to figure out how to come back to her old self, let alone move forward. All she could seem to do was go through the motions.

She'd had bad ends to relationships before, but nothing compared to the pain of losing Gerd, even for these two weeks. What if I lose her for good? she worried. I won't even think about that. It'll drive me crazy. I've got to concentrate on something else. Maybe I should go get something to eat. But I'm not hungry. When was I even hungry last? Why am I even thinking about eating? Hell, at least it would be something to do. But I don't want to do anything.

Just then, she heard the door to the theatre open behind her. She turned suddenly, startled that someone was there after all. It was Susan. Max realized she'd been staring at Susan's car in the parking lot, without even realizing it, the whole time she'd been sitting there.

"Max? What're you doing perched back here?"

"Nothing. What were you up to, repairs or laundry?"

"Repairs. Don't you remember Hannah's dress getting hung on the edge of that flat last night?"

Max shook her head.

"Well, it ripped like you wouldn't believe. I've spent an hour just getting it to hang right. Now I need sustenance. What about you? Could you use some sustenance?"

"Probably."

"Let's make that a yes."

They ended up on the patio at Hawkeye's Pub, because going to the Falafel Hut made Max think of Gerd. The September air was still pleasant. The tree leaves were green, but there was a hint of fall in the air thanks to the drop in temperatures and humidity. She was ready for jeans and sweaters, Max was thinking, but an Indian summer would probably creep in to throw her off kilter. Well, maybe that was fitting since she was so off kilter already.

"So, where do you think things stand with you and Gerd?" Susan asked as soon as the hostess left them to contemplate their menus.

"I don't know."

"You must have an inkling, Max."

Fiddling obsessively with the edge of her menu, Max wondered if she could avoid saying out loud what she'd been thinking since Gerd left her motel room. She sneaked a look at Susan. No, she couldn't get off the hook. "We're in trouble," she said finally. "There's a lot in our way and I don't think we know what to say to each other or how to change anything."

"Did you feel like she was choosing between you and her family?"

"Yeah, I did. If the situation had been different I would've done . . . or, well, I wouldn't have . . . what I mean is, if her brother weren't sick I wouldn't have tucked tail and run, you know?"

"I think I can understand that."

"But how can I be in the picture when no one but Gerd wants me there?"

"That's a good question."

"I mean, what am I supposed to say? 'I know your brother's hanging between life and death and your mother hates my guts but I still need some of your attention'? That's so selfish."

"So you didn't want to be demanding?"

"Of course not."

When the waitress came to take their orders, Susan said they needed more time. "Max, let me ask you something. Have you thought that by moving into that motel room . . . oh, for heaven's sake, Max, you know I heard about that . . . you were being just as demanding as you say you didn't want to be?"

"Excuse me?" Max said, looking pissed. "How do you figure that?"

"Gerd's brother is critically injured, right? That means she's got to put most of her concentration on him. But she's also at home part of the time, and that means she's got to concentrate on her parents. And she knows they're concentrating on her too, watching her, judging her, saving things to bring up later. They probably wouldn't even be speaking to each other if this hadn't happened to Gerald. Now factor into this that you went up with her. Why?"

"She wanted me to."

"Exactly. She needed your help with her brother and her

parents. She needed a support system. When you moved out you took that away from her, Max. You demanded her attention separately from everyone else, and she's not in a position to give that to you right now."

"But what about my position? I was staying in her parents' house and they didn't want me there. Don't I have to respect their feelings, especially considering they're a little on edge right now?"

"That doesn't matter."

"Gerd's mother probably wishes I could trade places with Gerald and be in the coma instead. How does that not matter, Susan?"

"Because she wanted to come between you and Gerd and you let her. Why should you respect her wishes when she got everything she wanted and you got nothing?"

"Shit." Max stared at the table for a long time. "I never thought of it this way."

Susan smiled. "You don't have as many years of experience to draw on as I do. You're young."

"And I'm pretty self-centered, too. Right?"

"Yes, you are. You haven't even tried to tell me that those many years of experience don't show on me at all."

"They don't," Max said lamely.

"Thank you. I do think that you're less self-centered than you used to be. And I also think that might keep improving if you stay with Gerd."

"I should go home and call her, huh?"

"I think so. But first, you'd better eat something. Do you have any idea how much weight you've lost?"

"No, why? Do I look thinner?"

"That's an understatement. Let's get a good nutritious meal into your system. Then you'll be ready to talk to Gerd."

Max reached across the table to squeeze Susan's hand. "Thank you. I'm not usually this grateful when someone points out my faults."

"Max, I love you and I'm glad I could help. I have one further piece of advice, though."

"What's that?"

"Don't get cocky now."

"Me?" Max protested, thinking that Susan knew her all too well.

"Yes, you. This isn't going to be easy. A few apologies aren't going to fix what's wrong. You need to back up your words with your actions, and it's going to be an uphill battle with those parents of hers."

"Believe me, Susan, even in all your wisdom, you only know the half of it."

As she slowed down, looking for the exit to the hospital, Max wondered if all the family would be there. After several phone calls sorting out what had gone sour, she was driving back to Richmond.

She'd told Gerd what Susan had helped her realize. "I let your mother come between us because part of me is scared of being involved in a committed relationship."

Gerd told Max what she'd had to figure out on her own. "I want acceptance from my parents and you even though I'm not willing to play it straight anymore."

What they'd decided was that separation wasn't the answer. When they were together the happiness far outweighed the heart-ache. When they were apart, it was just the reverse. "That means something, doesn't it?" Max had asked.

"It means that you should get your butt up here for a weekend," Gerd told her.

"It's on its way."

"Hey, Max, I'm really glad you're coming back."

"Me too, G. Me too."

This time she had agreed to stay at Gerd's parents' house. Gerd had told Ruth and Campbell that Max was coming up again. Then she'd very simply added that if Max wasn't welcome, she wouldn't be at home anymore either. They hadn't endorsed the arrangement but they also hadn't said no. Max knew this didn't mean they had accepted Gerd's being gay. But they weren't shutting off their communication and support anymore, so maybe little by little they'd become more tolerant. Max wasn't sure she ever wanted to . . . to what . . . be "friends" with them–well, not with Ruth anyway–but she would like to stay in their house at their invitation, rather than their surrender, someday.

And what about Gerald? Max wondered. How was he doing? Had there been any changes since last night? By the end of last week he'd been the same. Gerd and her father were wondering if they should keep him on the respirator, but her mother was adamant that given more time he'd wake up. Then this week he'd started showing signs that he might. Of course there were no guarantees, the doctors warned them. But he'd begun to move his arms and legs some, to make noises, open his eyes for a second, and Gerd said he'd squeezed her hand yesterday.

Max had sent a lot of positive thoughts his way. He was such a special person. She'd thought of him fondly since that first afternoon they'd bonded over football. He was loved and needed by a great many people. She just couldn't believe it was time for him to leave all that behind.

The hospital had moved Gerald into another room. Max was in such a rush that she forgot to ask where it was. Now she was trying to hurry down the hallway and look at each door too. Why hadn't she asked the nurse if she knew how he was doing?

There was his room. The door was slightly open but not enough so that she felt comfortable walking in. Max took a deep breath, then knocked.

"Come in," Ruth called.

As she did, Max saw a wonderful sight. Gerd was sitting beside Gerald's bed. There was no respirator. His eyes were open. Gerd's happy expression grew even happier as she turned toward Max.

Max was barely conscious of Ruth and Campbell sitting there. Her heart was pounding so hard she thought it was going to explode. Her knees felt weak. She was dizzy. Was this over seeing Gerald awake again?

"I'm so glad you're here, treat," Gerd said, coming over to her.

As Gerd wrapped her arms around her, the realization settled over Max like sinking into a warm bath. This is how love feels. I'm in love with this woman. Oh God. It was the most wonderful thing she had ever experienced. She pressed Gerd close to her, leaning her cheek against the top of her head and drinking in the smell of CK One. "Umm," she sighed, contented all the way down to her toes.

When she heard that, Gerd stirred, leaning back to glance up at Max. She knew what that kind of sigh meant. She just had to see Max's face, to see it in her eyes, to see her in love.

A smile spread so quickly over Max's face that she felt positively silly. She wrapped her arms more tightly around Gerd, leaning into her ear. "I love you," she whispered, brushing her lips against Gerd's curls.

"I love you too," Gerd whispered back, kissing Max's neck and sending shivers through every part of her. "Can you imagine any better sight than my little brother awake again?" she asked more loudly, letting Max go as she turned back toward Gerald's bed.

"No, I can't," Max assured her. Then she looked at Gerald. Tears filled her eyes. "Welcome back, Rip Van Winkle. It wasn't the same while you were napping."

Gerald's mouth moved very slowly until he got out a raspy "Thanks." As he smiled, Max felt her tears flow onto her cheeks. His eyes crinkled just like Gerd's.

As Max let go of Gerd to dab her eyes she saw everyone else was leaking tears as well. "Would you like a Kleenex?" Ruth asked her when she reached down to wipe her hand on her jeans.

It took Max a moment to answer. It was the first time Ruth had asked her something without an undertone of hostility. Not that it sounded particularly friendly, either, it just had the ring of a practical offer. But it was a step in a better direction. "Thanks, I could really use one," Max said.

Okay, so I love Gerd, Max thought. But that means I have to keep dealing with her family. Do I really want to be accepted by people that are so different from me? she wondered, wiping her eyes.

Looking back at Gerd, she felt giddy immediately. There was her answer. The Salon Visage haircut, the designer clothes and shoes, the gold charm bracelet, the BMW in the parking lot, none of these things excluded her from the love that shone out of those crinkling, electric blue eyes. And she returned that love, despite the difficulties she was sure they'd face, because she wanted to face them together.

About the Author

Angie Vicars has written many things for most of her life. Most recently, her work has appeared in Knoxville's free weekly paper, *Metro Pulse* <www.metropulse.com>. Angie also founded the Writers' Roundtable at Barnes & Noble, Knoxville, and holds an MFA in screenwriting from the University of Miami.